An Imperfect Reunion

Trina Lane

Published by Trina Lane

All Trademarks are the property of their respective owners

An Imperfect Reunion, Second Edition

Copyright © 2017, 2025 Trina Lane

Cover Art by Angela Haddon

Digtial ISBN: 978-1-967648-15-3

Paperback ISBN: 978-1-967648-16-0

About An Imperfect Reunion

♥

Their plans for a paradise vacation didn't include bullets and bombs.

The Boston crew booked the perfect escape—sun, surf, and Mai Tais on a remote tropical island. But before their vacation even begins, paradise is obliterated by a coordinated terrorist attack that shatters the island and scatters the friends into survival mode.

Cut off from each other and unsure who is alive, they must navigate explosions, chaos, and collapsing infrastructure to reunite. While the others fight their way back to one another, Ryan becomes central to the counter-operation as an unexpected asset in the hunt for the terrorists responsible.

As the attacks widen and the truth behind them unravels, the friends find themselves at the center of a plot designed to tear apart more than a single island. One meant to fracture a nation.

Now they have to answer a single question:

Is love—between partners, friends, and found family—strong enough to hold when the world is engineered to break it?

Chapter One

May

"**A**lannah Nicole McGuire!"

Calleigh stood with her arms crossed, tapping her foot and counted to ten under her breath while she waited for her five, almost six-year-old, daughter deign to grace her mother with her presence.

A pixie with a mop of curly black hair and sapphire eyes peered around the doorframe to her bathroom.

"Yeah?"

"Can you tell me why all my makeup is out and there is powder and eye shadow dust all over the vanity?"

"I was using it."

Of course. That makes perfect sense.

"Why? You know you're not supposed to go digging in your fathers' and my bathroom."

"But I needed it for our tea party."

She almost didn't want to know. Almost.

"Why did you need makeup for a tea party?"

Alannah blinked slowly, looking exactly like Rick when he was confused.

"Because we needed another girl."

Calleigh did some quick math in her head. Their house was bursting at the seams for the annual Memorial Day get-together. She knew that Mikey, Brandon and Deshawn were outside kicking the soccer ball around in the backyard. That left Charlie and Gabriella as Alannah's partners in crime.

"Can you show me?"

Alannah rolled her eyes, apparently assuming that her mother was too stupid to figure out the obvious logic of her mind. With enough sass to spare already in her young life, Calleigh sometimes dreaded the teenage years ahead of them, but their daughter held a special spirit that kept the household effervescent. They left the master bedroom and went down to the second floor, where the kids' and guest rooms were located. Alannah headed for her room, and Calleigh stepped into the best replication of a fairy princess forest outside of a Disney movie. She had to hold back the giggles at the sight that greeted her.

Poor little Charlie—Vic, Miranda and Chase's five-year-old—was sitting at the play table. He wore a gold plastic tiara, Alannah's bright pink Easter dress and a smile. Calleigh had to give her daughter credit on the makeup job, even if it looked as though the blush, eyeshadow and lipstick had been applied for an outlandish drag show event rather than a Sunday afternoon tea party.

"Wow," she drawled. "Charlie, sweetheart, are you okay?"

He nodded and picked up his teacup, pretending to take a drink. Gabriella poured some for Alannah, and the three of them carried on as if royalty were in residence.

"Oh, my God!"

Calleigh turned at the exclamation. Rick stood behind her, admirably trying to hold in the laughter that was pouring out of his eyes. "They're going to kill you."

She pushed him back a couple of feet so the kids weren't paying attention to them. "Oh no. That was all *your* daughter's doing."

"You're the one who showed her what makeup was."

Conor snuck up behind Rick and wrapped his arms around their husband's waist. "An' yisser the one who showed her de YouTube videos with makeup artists."

Rick groaned and leaned back against Conor's shoulder. "She kept asking me how the people in the circus got to be so colorful."

Calleigh gave both her husbands a quick kiss. "As much as I love seeing you two. Why are you here and not supervising Chase on the grill out back? You remember last fall when he turned the burgers into black briquettes?"

"He's safe. Grape-nuts and Logan are keeping an eye on him. It completely confounds me how a nationally renowned plastic surgeon utterly cannot work a basic grill."

Conor nibbled on Rick's ear. "I think he likes ter act de maggot so that everyone will take over an' he can be a total dosser with a drink an' snack, while de kip of us do all de work."

That is a rather genius idea.

"Hmm, like how the two of you are slaving away right now?"

"Hey, Miranda and Vic are getting the fruit salad together, Ryan's keeping an eye on the boys, and Clay told us to get out of the kitchen while he's finishing up the other stuff."

"Ah. So the two of you thought you'd sneak upstairs for a little playtime."

Rick pulled Calleigh into his arms and nuzzled her neck. "You could come with us," he whispered. "You know how I love being in the middle."

She gave Rick a quick grope and then stepped back.

"Tease."

She smiled. "Maybe, but in case you forgot," she pointed into the bedroom. "There are three other ankle-biters needing supervision. And maybe some wet wipes."

Rick and Conor both peered around the door, snickering. Rick pulled out his phone and snapped a photo of Charlie, then quickly sent the message to Vic.

About thirty seconds later, there was a shout from the floor below. Rick and Conor took off for the third floor as if fire licked at their heels.

"Cowards!" Calleigh called out.

She took one last look into the bedroom and decided to go face Charlie's parents. As she approached the kitchen, she heard Miranda, Vic, and Clay's excited voices.

"Is it safe to come in?" She called out.

Miranda came running over and gave Calleigh a tight hug. "Are you kidding me? This is the best blackmail material ever!"

Vic rolled his eyes. "While I can't say I'm as excited as my wife at seeing our son in pink crinoline, I will say he's showing off those legs as only a proud Burns man could."

Ryan looked up from mixing the bruschetta pasta salad. "I agree with Vic. Yellow is much more his color, or maybe a nice sunset orange."

Vic took the tray of extra-crispy seasoned fries from the oven. There would have been a mutiny from the kids had they only stuck with fruit and grilled veggies.

"You are so gay," Vic said.

"Says the man with a male lover of what, twenty-five years now?" Ryan countered.

Miranda stirred the lemonade in the big pitcher. "Um hello. Wife here? He swings both ways."

Ryan looked around the room. "Speaking of swinging, where did your two men go off to?"

Calleigh felt her cheeks heat, and Ryan chuckled.

"Never mind."

The door to the backyard opened, and Chase popped his head in. "Ethan and Logan said that the food is just about done." He was about to close the door when he peeked back in. "Oh, and Calleigh, I just wanted to let you know that the acoustics of your house are amazing. Sound from the third floor carries really well." He winked, then disappeared.

They all looked up at the ceiling.

"I'm going to kill them," Calleigh said softly.

She picked up the video monitor from the counter and hit the talk-over button. "Charlie, Gabriella, and Alannah, please come downstairs. Lunch is ready."

"But Mom, we're drinking our tea!"

Calleigh winced at the shout that came through the tiny speaker. None of the kids stood up or even appeared to contemplate her request.

She pushed the button. "Okay, I guess that means we get to eat all the hotdogs and French fries."

Suddenly it sounded like a herd of elephants was stampeding above their heads. Everyone in the room laughed. Calleigh picked up a couple of side dishes and carried them out to the picnic tables they had set up for the gathering. Mikey and Brandon had arranged the place settings earlier. She smiled as she noticed they'd used rocks from the garden to hold down the plates and napkins.

"Mikey, Brandon, thank you for setting the table!"

Mikey froze on the spot and put his hands on his waist. "I told you, it's Michael now. I'm too old for that baby name!"

"Right, sorry!"

"Jeez, Mom. Don't you know that ten-year-olds don't go by those silly kid names anymore?" Ethan asked with a smirk

A great cry from the yard assaulted her ears. Deshawn, Ethan and Ryan's son, stood in the goal holding up the soccer ball he'd just stopped. Brandon kneeled in the grass dramatically weeping as if he'd just lost the World Cup final.

"Nice stop D!" Ethan cheered.

"He looks good, Ethan."

"Yeah, he's worked really hard with the psychologist, and is opening up a lot more."

When they'd met seven years ago, Calleigh never would have pictured Ethan wearing a proud papa face. But when he and Ryan had announced a couple of years ago that they were adopting an eight-year-old out of foster care, it forced her to reevaluate her friend's personality. To her, Ethan had always been the margarita guzzling, smart-ass, hair band fan. Killer in the courtroom and jester in the living room.

There was also the matter of both Ethan and Ryan having been workaholics as long as she'd known them. Ethan was an assistant U.S. Attorney, and Ryan was now the special agent in charge of the FBI Boston division. She'd been slightly worried about how they would handle the demands of parenthood. But the men had seemed to blend the two parts of their lives with only moderate growing pains.

It certainly helped that Deshawn was a special kid. He'd been in the system for four years. Was gentle, imaginative and even-tempered. From the moment they'd introduced him to Michael and Brandon, the three boys had gotten along fantastically. She knew from Ryan's bragging that Deshawn did very well in school. Calleigh had seen the shy and very quiet little boy blossom under his parents' praise, and he now expressed himself well.

"Has he seen his sisters lately?"

Ethan frowned and shook his head. "We tried setting up a playdate with their foster parents a couple of weeks ago, but got a call that they couldn't make it. We try to make sure they talk on the phone once a week. I'm hoping they find a forever home soon."

"Would the two of you ever consider taking them in?"

He sighed. "I don't think we could. I mean, we love Deshawn. He's really completed our family, but having a matching set of six-year-old girls too?" He gave a little shudder. "I would have no idea what to do with them."

Rick pushed between them and snagged a grape from the fruit salad bowl. "Twins. Double the trouble, double the fun. Believe me, we know."

"*Mo grian! Mo gealach!* Bring ya' in!" Conor called out. "Where is de bag of taytos an' black stuff?"

Rick handed Conor a glass of water and a skewer of grilled veggies. "No chips or Guinness. We're going healthy. Remember?"

"*Gabh síos ort fhéin*" Conor said under his breath.

"If I could I would, but that's what I have you for love."

Rick bent over, and Calleigh couldn't help but stare at her husband's ass. It was still as tight as the photos she'd seen of his days as a collegiate soccer player. She glanced up and saw Conor's eyes also trained on the defined globes. Their gazes met, and in the aquamarine depths Calleigh saw the promise of a pleasurable evening once their house had cleared out for the night.

"All right, you three. Don't make me get the hose out," Chase said as he set a platter of meat on the table.

Rick handed Conor a bottle of Guinness with a chaste kiss. "That's because I love you."

"Mmhm, and you don't want to listen to him bitch all night." Chase said.

They all piled food on their plates and found a seat around the table. Miranda and Vic were the last to sit down after making sure the kids table was settled.

"So I've been thinking." Ryan said.

"Always dangerous," Chase mumbled.

Ryan glanced around before flipping Chase the finger, while taking a drink to hide the gesture from little eyes.

"It's been a long time since we took a vacation." He looked over at Ethan and saw a nod. "I don't know about all of you, but with work and kids and life, it's been four years for us. I haven't heard about any of you making any big plans."

A chorus of heads shook around the table.

"Well, except for Niall, Trevor, and Matt. I swear, those three take a vacation at least every six months."

"Three incomes and no kids. Plus, Niall travels for his work a lot, so they like to take weekend trips around his shoots." Logan added.

"I get it. Where are they, by the way?"

"Matt texted a little bit ago. They're on the way. Apparently, Trevor had a slight mishap in the shower."

"Is he okay?" Miranda asked.

Logan snickered. "Yeah. Apparently he fell on Niall's—Ow!" He shouted and rubbed his leg. "I was going to say tile you perve." He said to Clay.

"Yeah, sure you were."

Ryan rolled his eyes. "Anyway. So, Ethan and I have been tossing around the idea of planning a much-needed vacation for a while, and we thought we'd ask if any of you were interested in putting something together?"

"A group vacation kind of thing. Sort of like when Rick, Calleigh, and Conor tied the knot." Ethan added.

The table was quiet for a moment.

"Well ... I have some time due to me at the hospital," Miranda said.

"And I make my own schedule." Chase added.

They looked over at Vic, who nodded. "Depends on how long we're talking, but I could probably swing coverage."

Ethan clapped. "That's two groups out of five. Who else is in?"

Calleigh glanced at both Rick and Conor, who nodded. She'd only ever taken time off when they ended up with a sick kid, and she'd built up some vacation time since going back to work three years ago.

They'd initially planned on her staying home until Alannah started kindergarten, but after two years she'd told her men that she was going nuts and needed to get back into the operating room. She'd spent too many years working her ass off to become a nurse anesthetist to forgo the profession she loved. Her two software specialists had made the switch from the sports video game company they had worked at when the three of them had met, to one that specialized in multi-player online role-playing games. Their company even branched out into the development of virtual reality games that became so popular in the last several years. The diversified platforms assured them steady work and competitive income. Which was the primary reason they'd been able to afford their forever home in the coveted Bellevue Hill area last year.

"We're in." They announced together.

Ethan looked over at Clay and Logan. "How about you two?"

"Vacation time isn't an issue, but you know how things are at the department. We'll have to see if it's possible." Clay said.

"Let's get this party started!" Trevor called out as he, Matt, and Niall came into the backyard.

Logan startled, and Calleigh watched as Clay assessed his husband's mental space. Logan had made successful strides over the years in his battle with PTSD, but there were times environmental events triggered him.

"Fashionably late again, Trev?" Chase asked.

Trevor shrugged. "Hey, it's a holiday. I had people to do and things to see." He sat down in one of the empty spots. "What were you talking about?"

"Going on a group vacation, and I'm pretty sure you have the same priorities every day, not just on national holidays." Clay said.

Trevor put down his bottle of water. "Well, when you're as lucky as I am, and get to wake up next to the worlds sexiest two men then I figure being a few minutes late to a family barbecue because of some extracurricular fun is not only understandable, but frankly expected."

Calleigh snickered as Trevor stared each of them down one by one with a raised eyebrow. As each person at the table nodded, Trevor's smirk got bigger and bigger.

"Good, now that we are all in agreement that I have the best sex life on the planet, I can share my other good news. I've already cleared it with the captain."

"Cleared what?" Logan asked.

"I talked to the captain earlier this week after Ethan had called me to brainstorm. You and I are scheduled to train some minions for vacation coverage, anyway. As long as they pass muster, a few days off would be a perfect test. He made me promise we would come back though."

"As if you would ever give up all those toys you get to play with." Logan said.

"My precious." Trevor said with a sigh.

"Do you need a minute?" Clay asked.

"Oh no. I'm good."

"Yes, *Bello* you are." Matt kissed the top of his head before sitting down.

Ethan stood up. "So that's it? We're all in?"

Rick nodded. "God help the world, but it sounds like we are. Now, have we considered the logistics of thirteen adults and six kids all traveling concurrently to the same location?"

"And exactly where and when are we going to attempt to pull this off?" Vic asked.

"That's what today is all about," Ethan said.

Logan set down his fork. "Hmm, and here I thought today was about paying our respects to those who have given the ultimate sacrifice for our country."

Clay squeezed Logan's shoulder, then leaned in and said something softly. Calleigh watched as Logan's shoulders lost their tension. Logan was a former Ranger and Ryan had served in the Navy before joining the FBI. However, Logan's experience had differed greatly from Ryan's. She knew he'd seen and done things that irrevocably changed him. He'd come a long way with professional help over the years, but sometimes there were still shadows in his eyes. Logan's hearing loss was a daily reminder of the head trauma he'd experienced as a result of the attack that had killed his most of his team.

Calleigh looked over at her sons. Their biological father, Kevin, had died while deployed when the boys were only babies. Ten years may have passed, but she still felt a pang in her heart when she thought about how he'd never gotten a chance to meet the boys. Rick, Conor, and herself attempted to include Kevin's memory in the boys' lives, but sometimes Calleigh felt it was more for her benefit than theirs. In fact, they were going to the Massachusetts National Cemetery on Cape Cod tomorrow to pay their respects.

"Sorry guys. Didn't mean to kill the mood."

Chase shook his head. "Nothing to apologize for, Logan. You're right about today, but I also think of it as an opportunity to celebrate and be thankful for their service. How that sacrifice allows all of us to gather here together, stuff ourselves with barbecue, and watch our children play without worrying about stepping on an IED and getting blown to bits. What you and your brothers and sisters have done will never be forgotten by any of us here."

Logan nodded and smiled. "So where are we all headed? The Caribbean? Swiss Alps? Mexico?"

"Disney World!" All the kids screamed.

"No!" All the adults responded.

Charlie, being the youngest, cried. Vic quickly stood and went to settle his son down. After about twenty seconds, he returned with a pained expression on his face.

"I sort of promised him we'd take them to Disney World another time."

"He totally has you wrapped around his finger." Chase said, laughing.

Miranda stared Chase down. "Like Gabriella isn't daddy's little princess?"

Chase shrugged. "Don't think you're innocent here."

"Yeah, but she's mom." Calleigh said.

Miranda nodded. "Thank you. Moms get a permanent pass for babying their children as long as they live. I don't care if he's three or thirty-three."

"Anyway!" Trevor shouted. "How about someplace totally exotic? Like ... Fiji!"

"How about somewhere affordable? Like Wyoming?" Clay suggested.

Everyone at the table turned to look at him.

"What I've always wanted to ride a horse?"

Conor leaned in and looked down the table. "If we are really doin' this. It shouldn't be 'alf assed. What aboyt somethin' like dat movie?"

"Adventures in Babysitting?" Miranda suggested.

"Weekend at Bernie's?" Chase added.

"RV?" Rick chimed.

"Hostel?" Logan asked.

Trevor raised his hand. "Mr. Hobbs Takes A Vacation?"

Conor stood up. "Go an' shoite! I'm talkin' aboyt de one where they go al' over Europe."

"EuroTrip? Funny as fuck, but I don't think that's exactly family friendly." Rick said.

"No, I think he means the National Lampoon's one." Vic said.

Conor nodded while Calleigh and Miranda rapidly shook their heads.

"There is no way in hell I'm making a multiple-destination trip with all the kids. Can you imagine the ... Oh God I can't even begin to say what could go wrong." Calleigh said.

Conor's face drained of color. "Sorry *ár ghrá*. I wasn't thinkin'."

Calleigh patted his hand. "It's okay. All right. So we want somewhere exotic, fun, relatively easy to travel to and from and not a place we'll have to take out a second mortgage to achieve."

All the heads nodded.

"Hawaii?" Niall said, softly.

Everyone turned to look at the man who had said nothing since he'd nodded his greeting upon arrival.

Ethan tilted his head. "Huh. Never would have thought of ... Well if we ... that just might work."

Chapter Two

♥

E than leaned in closer to his laptop screen, squinting. He did not need reading glasses. Nope. No Siree. Ugh! This was the whole reason he'd had LASIK done. So he wouldn't have to keep using glasses and contacts. But, reading glasses meant getting old, and he was *not* old.

"Is that an 'R' or a 'P'?"

"E, what are you working on?"

"I'm looking at vacation packages, trying to figure out if we'd all be better off if we used an agency with a pre-planned package or just made our own itinerary."

"How did you get elected to be the organizer of this circus?"

Ethan shrugged. "Well, it was kind of our..." he looked up at Ryan and smiled. "Okay, my idea. And somebody had to take charge; otherwise, it really would be a three-ring circus. I just plan on putting together some proposals, then the group can vote on their favorite. I want to make sure there's stuff to keep the kids entertained, but not drive Logan, Clay, Trevor, Matt, and Niall nuts."

Ryan rubbed Ethan's shoulders. Strong fingers dug into the muscles that felt strung as tight as violin strings. Ethan let out a groan and leaned into the impromptu massage.

"God, please don't stop."

Ryan's warm breath blowing over his ear made Ethan shiver. "That's what you said the other night."

"That's what I'll say every night given the chance." He spun in his chair and wrapped his arms around Ryan's waist, nuzzling the still taut stomach.

At forty-four, his husband now spent more time behind a desk than he did out in the field, and while his waistline might be a little thicker than it was when they had met, it was still firm.

In truth, Ethan was happy that Ryan was now in a supervisory role rather than a field agent. After the two of them successfully got a conviction on the man who'd orchestrated Ethan's attack six years ago, Ryan had made a shift from the division of economic espionage to the special security branch-terrorism unit. He'd been in the thick of the investigation when a mass casualty event occurred downtown three years ago. And while Ethan would never even think of holding Ryan back, he'd had enough terror in his life. Not that any FBI job was exactly safe, but there was graduating levels of exposure to daily threats.

"I don't like seeing you work this hard for a vacation, E."

"I just want to make sure everything goes perfectly. Don't forget this is going to be Deshawn's first vacation ever."

"I know, now I want you to save whatever spreadsheet you've been categorizing and come to bed. I plan on making you beg me not to stop a lot more tonight."

"Hmmm. Deshawn's asleep?"

"Yes, now I want you naked and hard by the time I get out of the shower."

Ethan didn't even think twice about closing his browser window. His cock was already filling with thoughts of what Ryan had in store for him. The lights of Boston's North End glowed outside the arched windows of their loft. He'd loved this space from the moment he'd seen it on the computer, and when they'd stepped through the private entrance elevator for the first time he'd known this loft was destined to be their home.

Not that he didn't trust his husband, but Ethan still opened the door to his son's room just enough to peek in and make sure that Deshawn was sound asleep. He smiled at the multitude of moons and stars being projected onto the ceiling from the little LED globe they'd gotten off Amazon. Deshawn might be ten years old, but he hadn't been afforded much security in his brief life. If the night light made him feel safe in his own home, then Ethan was all for it. He closed the door, making sure the click of the latch was as soft as possible.

He saw Ryan's shadow through the curtained glass French doors of their master suite. Ethan seized the moment as his husband went to the bathroom. He dashed into the bedroom and stripped all his clothes. Despite the urgency, he couldn't bring himself to abandon his clothes on the floor. So he did the next most irresponsible thing and draped them over the chair. A short time later, the sound of water hitting the floor of the shower stall made Ethan's cock stand up and beg like a starving puppy.

He groaned. Ryan was torturing him on purpose, the sexy bastard. He sat up and smiled. Who said he had to wait for his treat? He went into the bathroom and opened the glass shower door. Ryan faced away from him, but a flex of the muscles in his back meant he knew Ethan had invaded their second favorite place to make love since Deshawn had joined their household. Fortunately, the shower was plenty big enough for extracurricular activities. Their days of spontaneous fucking on the living room sofa and kitchen counters may have disappeared, but when they found the time and energy to make love, the passion was stronger than ever.

He spun Ryan around and dropped to his knees, taking Ryan's already hard cock in his mouth. Ryan's groan mingled with the sound of the water falling from the multiple jets, and Ethan slipped into his calming center where his brain turned off and his heart and instincts took over. Ethan sucked hard as Ryan gently gripped his head. He loved it when Ryan dragged his fingers through his hair. There was always just the right mix of soothing massage and spike of lust that went straight to his cock. He cupped Ryan's balls with one hand and the base of his cock with the other. Ethan mentally cheered when the muscles in Ryan's thighs twitched with the effort of keeping him upright. He pulled back, keeping his suction while dragging his tongue up the length of Ryan's cock, tracing the heavy vein that pulsed with life. Ryan's cock swelled, and Ethan groaned, anticipating the flavor of Ryan's release sliding over his tongue. He slid his mouth up and down Ryan's length, pressing him deep into his throat and inhaling the freshly washed scent of his husband's groin. Ethan pulled back to catch some air and was rewarded with the taste of pre-cum. A delicacy unlike any other in his life. He lapped at the tip, teasing Ryan into giving him some more before sinking all the way back to the base while massaging his balls.

"Oh, fuck. E."

His hands and mouth found the rhythm that Ryan loved best. Ethan was the maestro of this interlude, though. His heart raced, and blood surged with the power of having Ryan's body under his control. He ran his tongue around the head every few strokes. Ryan's cock became slick with saliva, and Ethan's hand jacked Ryan's shaft while he hummed. Ryan's fingers twisted in his hair, and Ethan's throat burned in the best way as his hips thrust.

"Christ, you just keep getting better, baby. I love the way you suck my cock. Love the way you take such good care of me."

Ethan's heart and cock throbbed with Ryan's words. His blood rushed, making every nerve ending fire and lightning bolt sensations course throughout his body.

He savored Ryan's pre-cum, desperate for every little taste of his husband's pleasure. Ethan knew Ryan was getting close by the way his hips moved, his grip in Ethan's hair grew stronger and his needy moans echoed in the tiled space. He hummed in triumph as Ryan's body shook and his cock swelled.

Ryan jerked out of Ethan's mouth, and it took a second for his lust-fogged brain to catch up.

"Wha—"

"Not tonight, baby. I've been dreaming of coming in that tight ass all day."

Ethan stood and turned away, presenting Ryan with the object of his desire. He expected to hear the click of the lube and the stroke of Ryan's fingers inside him, but Ethan found his brain scrambled once again when Ryan spun him around and his back hit the wall. Ryan's heavy body pressed hard against him, and their wet skin slid together.

"Brace your leg up on my hip."

Ryan's deep voice sounded raw. Ethan wrapped his leg around Ryan's waist, pressing his calf against the curve of Ryan's ass. Ryan reached between Ethan's thighs, and he slid his slick fingers over the patch of skin beneath his sac, reaching farther back until they circled around his hole. God, this never got old. Ryan's fingers pushed their way through, Ethan's body opening eagerly at the familiar touch. Ethan rolled his head against the wall, while his hands gripped Ryan's shoulders. His cock throbbed with the need to come, but he never wanted to rush their time together. They had precious little of it.

"Ry, Ry I need."

"I know, baby. I'm going to fill you up with my cock just as soon as you're ready." He pushed a third finger inside, and Ethan moaned long and low with the stretch. "That's it, E. Your ass is so hungry for my cock. It's going to feel so tight and hot around me. I'm going to fuck you so good and fill you with my come."

Ryan's long fingers moved in and out relentlessly, spreading lube and stretching him until Ethan mentally begged.

"God, fuck, do it!" he shouted as the mental block crumbled. He gripped Ryan hard, trying to bring him in closer with his leg.

"Gotta slick myself, baby. Won't hurt you no matter how desperate we are."

He heard Ryan gasp and opened his eyes briefly to see his husband slicking up his cock with the lube. The darkened flesh shiny. Ryan backed him tighter against the wall. Ryan reached down and lifted each of Ethan's legs over his arms. His fingers dug into the flesh of Ethan's ass cheeks.

He wrapped his arms around the shoulders that sometimes carried the weight of the world, and kissed the pulsing vein on Ryan's neck. Ryan teased him by dragging his cock along the cleft of his ass before the head nudged at his hole. Ryan thrust his hips forward, pushing past the muscled ring of Ethan's opening. The familiar slight sting was welcome before the heavy shaft once again filled him in a way that only Ryan could. With each shuttle of his husband's cock, Ethan sensed the fibers of their bond tighten. He clutched at Ryan's shoulders, whispers of love getting lost in the sound of heavy water falling around them. His hole stretched wide around Ryan's width. Ryan's hips met his ass with every thrust. He knew he had to be getting heavy. He knew they couldn't keep this up much longer. It wasn't as if they were in their twenties. But damned if he didn't wish his husband had some kind of supernatural strength to fuck him against the wall for hours.

As if Ryan read his thoughts, Ethan groaned when his husband's frantic thrusts slowed, dragging out each push and pull to their maximum limit. Ethan clenched around Ryan's cock with every powerful thrust of his hips. He cried out when Ryan bit down on his shoulder. Their bodies, slick with sweat and water, slid against one another. His dick ached as Ryan fucked him with slow, powerful thrusts.

"Every time, E. Every time it gets better."

He chuckled. "We must be somewhere around supercalifragilistic-expialidocious by now."

Ryan laughed. "God damnit. If you can say that word, I'm not doing something right."

He became incapable of speech as Ryan kicked into high gear again. Ethan arched his back and pushed down against Ryan's hips. He called on every yoga class he'd ever tried and brought his legs up closer to his chest, causing Ryan's cock to slide deeper into his ass. The deeper nerve endings cried out in joy at the attention, and Ryan growled. Actually growled. Their bodies collided each time Ryan shoved his cock into Ethan's ass. In contrast, Ryan nuzzled Ethan's cheek. His lips trailed little kisses along Ethan's neck and nibbled at the corner of his mouth.

"You ready to come, E? You gonna give it all up to me? Let me watch the come shoot out of your cock and land all over me?"

His control had reached the point of no return. "Yes, yeah ... just don't ... stop ... oh God, Ry!"

He wrapped his fingers around his straining cock, strangling a cry as a rush of ecstasy shot all the way from the tip of his toes to the top of his head. He squeezed and stroked, panting and chest heaving as this body raced towards orgasm.

"That's it, baby. You're getting close. I can feel your ass rippling around my cock. Fuck it feels so good."

Ethan shut his eyes as tiny explosions in his brain made him hit the back of his head against the tile. His throat became raw with guttural shouts before Ryan captured his mouth with his to silence the evidence of their activity. All the muscles in his body spasmed as the first shot of cum ejected from his dick. He jacked his cock, painting Ryan's chest and stomach with pearlescent seed.

Warmth flooded him as Ryan's frame became rigid and Ethan clutched his husband's head against his shoulder. The adrenaline from their arousal waned, and Ethan feared he'd end up on the floor with bruises not attributable to passion.

Can you say mood killer?

He gingerly put his legs down, wincing only slightly as his hip popped.

Nope not twenty, but so fucking worth it. He snickered. *Or maybe so worth the fucking is more appropriate.*

Ryan swayed a little, and Ethan managed to get him turned around so they could do one last rinse. Thank god for tankless water heaters. A quick dry and shuffle to the bedroom. Then bliss as he snuggled into Ryan's arms and floated on a cloud of Tempurpedic awesomeness.

"Love you, Ethan," Ryan mumbled

"Love you, too."

Chapter Three

July

L ogan slid the magazine of the Smith and Wesson Performance Center 1911 into the grip, checked the safety, and chambered a round. He pushed the button that turned on a light outside his door to alert anyone walking by that he was firing a weapon. A short walk over to the firing station put him in front of a small table. He removed his processors, picked up his safety glasses, then picked the weapon back up.

"Firing two!" he shouted.

He flipped the safety off, then positioned the muzzle into the port, squeezing the trigger twice. Even though he couldn't hear the sound of the shots, he felt the vibrations travel up his arm and the percussion wave hit his chest. Logan released the magazine and set the weapon back on the tray. He retrieved the bullets and casings, then set them in the designated inspection area he previously labeled. Next, he picked up a Beretta 92 FS 9mm that the crime scene techs retrieved a short distance from a murder scene yesterday.

As he picked up some ammo from his supply to load the magazine, the lamp on his table started flashing. He looked towards the closed glass door of his workspace. Trevor stood on the other side, pushing the doorbell. The flashing light served as an alert system in case he had his processors off.

He watched Trevor's lips move through the glass.

"What?"

Trevor kept talking and making gestures. He opened the door and walked in, speaking the entire time.

"Your tongue is ashy?"

Trevor put his fists on his hips and shook his head.

"Try again." Logan said. He watched while Trevor spoke. "You swallowed a penny?"

Trevor started signing. *"Did you see the email?"*

Logan signed back. *"Just screwing with you. Knew what you said. And no, haven't looked at email."*

Along with most of his immediate group of friends, Logan started taking American Sign Language classes a couple of years ago. Trevor and Clay were the most proficient, but they all tried, and that really meant a lot to him.

"Go look! Ethan sent the options to vote on."

Logan looked around the room. *"Some of us have work to do."*

Trevor shook his head and help up his phone. *"Put your toys down for one minute. We have more important things to discuss."*

Trevor's signing always got fast, and a bit jumbled when he got excited. Logan smiled and secured the weapon before turning to continue the conversation.

"Says the man I have to drag away from his equipment at the end of each shift."

"That's different. My stuff is totally awesome! Yours is just loud. Good thing you can't hear."

Logan watched Trevor's shoulders shake with laughter. Had someone said that to him six years ago, he probably would have lost his shit, or slipped into another flashback of the attack that had caused him to lose his hearing. However, Logan had come a long way, with the help of his therapist, in accepting the loss of his hearing and becoming an active member in the hard-of-hearing community.

He slipped his processors back on and gestured for Trevor to come closer. The second the magnet made a connection with the implant beneath his scalp, it was as if the world woke up. The immediate presence of sound, even in a quiet room, was both a little jarring and welcome.

"You on the air yet?"

"Yes, smartass. So what's so damn important that I have to look at this email right now?"

"It's a magical trip to the paradise of the pacific! Why wouldn't you want to look? I've been practically bouncing in circles waiting to hear something."

"I thought I told you to lie off the Monster drinks."

Trevor's expression turned into a mask of horror, and Logan snickered.

"Blasphemy! Now look here." Trevor pulled out his phone. "I was really hoping that Ethan would have some options that would appeal to those of us without rug rats running around. Don't get me wrong; I love all the kids. Well, most of them anyway." He smiled and winked.

"I hear you. It's going to be hard to make everyone in a group our size happy every day, but I think if anyone can pull off a plan, it'll be Ethan."

"It looks like he's put together options for the various islands."

Logan looked down at the screen of Trevor's phone. It was a whole lot bigger than his. Of course his phone was four years old, but he couldn't justify spending the money on a new one if his still worked.

"Here's a seven-day all-inclusive package for the big island. Looks nice. Has a variety of excursions to choose from each day. We could either match, or I guess pick different activities for some alone time."

"I've always wanted to see Kilauea. He included an eleven day four island hopper too." Trevor said.

"I've heard that Kauai is really nice. Wouldn't mind spending ten days exploring its secrets. I guess we'll just have to see how everyone votes. Did you turn in your PTO request yet?" Logan asked.

"Yeah, the captain wished us a good trip, but also managed to not so subtly remind me that this is a once in a lifetime allowance." Trevor gasped. "You think it might be possible that the BPD appreciates the squints that actually get them the test results they need for their super important I must have that info now cases?"

Logan chuckled. "I'd just keep an eye out for any voodoo dolls in the coming months. We don't want anything to jinx this vacation. I know you, Matt and Niall have done some traveling, but this is my first trip since that last deployment."

Trevor put his hand on Logan's shoulder. "Just a little different, huh?"

"Yeah ... a little."

He felt a familiar depression cloud float overhead, but forced it back by thinking of soaking up some sun on the beach with Clay, or maybe scuba diving. Who knew what misadventures they'd find? A knock on the large viewing window had both men looking up to see the head of forensics staring them down.

"Oh-oh. Better get back to work. Text me tonight with your vote, and I'll let you know what we decide." Trevor said.

"Why not just wait till the poll closes?"

"Because I gotta know!"

Logan shook his head as Trevor ran back across the hall to his AV suite, where he analyzed all the audio and video evidence the investigators brought him pertaining to active cases. And if they occasionally used the lunch hour to watch a movie on the massive projection wall, then nobody needed to know.

He went back over to his loading station and picked up the Beretta. The pistol felt very familiar in his hand as it wasn't too different from the M9 that he'd used in service. A sea of sand and the rat-a-tat-tat of automatic fire flickered through his brain. He set the weapon down and breathed slowly until the miniature flashback faded. At least he was no longer an emotional slave to the images and sounds. He'd tried so hard over the past six years to move forward after his medical discharge.

He'd planned to make a life as a Ranger, but the universe had had other ideas for him. Not that he wasn't happy. Because he was, most of the time. He had a husband and best friend that he loved with everything in him; he had a great job, an amazing group of friends, but PTSD was a cold-hearted bitch that wouldn't let go of his leg even after all this time. He'd spent thousands of hours in therapy, first with Matt, then with another therapist after his and Matt's friendship became too personal. But now and then, that bitch gave him a little reminder of the demons that followed him home.

When Ethan brought up the idea of a group vacation at the picnic, Logan had perked up. He and Clay had actually been saving their pennies for a big trip as they had never taken a honeymoon. While he was sure the two of them would find some time to sneak off together, he couldn't think of anything more he'd rather do than go on an adventure with those who had made his life worth living again.

But first there were guns to fire, tool marks to examine, and a whole lot of paperwork to do so bad guys got their due in court. He slid the casing into the magazine and smiled at the familiar click.

"Say hello to my little friend."

Niall opened the front door and stepped inside the loft home he shared with Matt and Trevor. It had been a very long day at the shoot, and all he wanted was a glass of wine and a quiet evening with one or both of his men wrapped around him. He set his satchel with his laptop and folder full of proofs from the day on the kitchen island. When he'd dropped off his equipment at the studio, he'd taken the time to run off the proofs, even though his eyes burned with exhaustion from looking through the viewfinder all day. He really should review them so he'd know what areas they needed to focus on tomorrow—but later. Maybe. If he found the energy.

As a fine art photographer, he rarely did commercial shoots, but when Nike had approached him about doing a campaign that took their advertising to another artistic level, he found himself intrigued. Niall relished a challenge, but days like today reminded him why he loathed corporate work. The manager of the campaign had been up in his business all day, telling him how something was supposed to look and what angle they wanted. Niall had finally had to tell him that if they wanted to take the photographs, they were welcome to. Too bad he'd waited almost five hours into the day to make his voice heard. Maybe tomorrow will be smoother now that he established boundaries.

He opened the built-in wine cooler and retrieved a bottle of Antica Napa Valley cabernet sauvignon. He set the bottle on the concrete countertop and turned to face the modular cabinet that contained all their kitchen supplies. A few seconds later, he had three wine glasses and the bottle opener in hand. When the cork popped, and he took a sniff, the first layers of stress fell away from his shoulders.

"I thought I heard you come in."

Niall looked up and found Matt walking towards him from the hallway that led to their bedroom. The sight of his tall Italian soothed his tired psyche. Matt's hair had gotten a little grayer in the past year, but in Niall's opinion it only made his green eyes stand out that much more. It was hard to believe that they were both over forty now, but ever since he'd found the men destined for him, Niall's soul felt years younger. Plus, it helped that they worked hard to maintain a healthy lifestyle. It had taken him long enough to find the men of his heart. He had no intention of leaving this earth—by abusing the flesh he had been given—sooner than when the great creator Manto called to him.

Matt stepped up behind him, and Niall relaxed back into his lover's embrace. This was his home. All that was missing was—

The front door swung open, and Trevor sauntered in.

"Hey guys. Is this a party of two, or can I join the festivities?"

Niall turned and opened his arms. Only a few seconds passed before Trevor's head rested on his chest. He kissed the soft blond hair and rubbed his lithe back. Niall frowned when he felt Trevor's ribs. Trevor had always been smaller than Matt and himself, but there was thin and then there was skinny. When they'd first met, Trevor had been skinny. Living on cans of soup in a tiny Dorchester apartment, but over the last five years they'd taught Trevor the joy of delicious foods not made of processed crap in tin cans.

"Thank you loves, this is exactly what I needed."

Trevor nuzzled against Niall's chest. "Rough day? I know this was different for you."

"Hmm, yes. Back when I was still trying to build up my reputation, I would take commercial jobs all the time, but I've been my own man for a long time now, and I'd forgotten what it's like. I'm blessed to have achieved recognition as an artist and honored they sought me out, but you know sometimes personalities just don't mix."

Matt angled Niall's head and kissed him. His lips said more than a whole dictionary of words.

"Let's take the wine into the bedroom. I can give you a massage, and while you're taking a quick rest, we'll cook." Matt looked down at Trevor. "Well, I'll cook and Trevor can keep me company."

Matt was the master chef of the house, although Trevor could whip up a mean grilled cheese and tomato soup when the occasion called for it. They gathered up their glasses, and Trevor grabbed the bottle of wine. Together they headed into the sanctuary of their room, where they'd spent many nights wrapped in each other's arms.

Since the morning Niall had woken from a dream in which the Great Spirit had shown him Matt and Trevor's images, it had taken a lot of hard work to blend their three lives. First, they'd had to deal with Trevor's kidnapping, then the trial. Trevor was Mr. Independent, and Matt had spent a lot of time teaching Niall that Trevor would become a part of them in his own way, at his own speed. Five years later, Niall knew they were exactly where they were supposed to be. What the future would hold was unknown, but he had enough trust in the universe to know that they would greet her together.

They each stripped until nothing separated their bodies but space, and Niall hoped that too would soon disappear. Matt poured them each a glass of wine, and Niall climbed onto the platform bed. He relaxed against the leather-padded headboard and lifted his arm. Trevor snuggled up against him. The golden hour light slanting through the windows of their loft made his shutter finger twitch at the sight of Matt standing nude before them. He clinked his glass with Trevor, and the two of them drank while watching Matt walk around the room, lighting a few candles. Matt may have been starting to show his years in some places, but certainly not in the hard sculpted body they currently feasted their eyes upon. His long cock showed signs of waking.

"Are you thinking what I'm thinking?"

"Holy fuck," Trevor whispered.

Matt smiled at them as he stood beside the bed. He sat down and bent over to kiss Niall's scars from the attack so many years ago. Niall held Matt's head to his chest and groaned when Trevor encircled his cock in a firm grip.

"I thought I was going to get a massage?"

Trevor grinned. "Haven't you heard of the happy ending massage?"

Matt attached his lips to Niall's nipples and flicked his tongue back and forth, while Trevor stroked his cock with his expert touch. Niall's fingers went lax on the glass of wine, but before it could fall to the floor, Matt took the glass, and he heard a soft clink as he set on the floating bedside table. Niall rolled on top of Trevor, and his lover arched up against him. They'd tried so many things over the years, but Niall's favorite was still being in the middle of his two men. Possessing Trevor's body and having Matt slide deep inside him.

Matt used his large hands to massage Niall's tension-filled muscles. Niall's arms almost collapsed when a particular knot uncoiled. Matt moved his hand down to the globes of Niall's ass and prepared him.

Niall let out a deep guttural moan as he kissed Trevor while he ground their cocks together. Trevor dug his fingers into Niall's hair. Niall still kept it long, and the little sting added another layer of pleasure.

Trevor forced Niall's head to the side and nibbled on his neck. Niall pushed back against Matt's finger entering him. He needed more.

"Fuck me, Niall," Trevor whispered in his ear.

"Give me that lube," he growled at Matt.

The emptiness he felt as Matt withdrew from his body had Niall stuttering for a breath. He quickly squeezed the tube and got to work stretching Trevor for a good hard fuck. With one finger inside, Niall sighed as Trevor's smooth hot walls clenched around him.

"You know I fucked him in the shower this morning. He shouldn't need too much stretching."

Niall looked down at Trevor. "He did?"

Trevor nodded quickly.

"Was it good?"

"Al ... oh god right there ... always. He gets so deep, and he's so strong he can just pick me up and shove me right down on that big cock."

"Jesus, Trev. I can picture it in my head."

"You need it, don't you, Niall. You need that big cock inside you right now," Trevor said.

"Yes," he groaned.

Trevor looked over Niall's shoulder. "Open him up, Matt. I bet he feels so tight and hot. I bet he's massaging your finger right now, his ass gripping and pulling it deeper. It's hungry."

Niall shook harder with each of Trevor's words. He maintained enough brain function to make sure his lover was ready before he pushed his cock against the stretched ring of muscle. He slipped just the head inside. The heat seared his bare flesh. He tried to slow down his breathing and concentrate on not plunging into Trevor with animalistic fervor. The crown of Matt's cock pushed against his hole, and Niall sucked in a breath at the beautiful surge of emotion that always flared between him and his soul mates. As one unit, they moved. Matting filled him with every thick inch and Trevor's ass gripped his cock. Matt finally snugged his hips up against Niall's ass. God his lover, reached deep inside him. Touched his heart and body in a way no other man ever had or ever could.

How many words have we said to each other over the years to express what sharing this intimacy means to us?

He looked deep into Trevor's eyes and realized that words were no longer necessary. Every emotion, every desire was right there shining bright through those azure windows. Trevor pulled his head down and their lips sealed their commitment. Their tongues danced, and Niall gathered Trevor in his arms right as Matt pressed his chest against Niall's back. Matt placed his lips against the back of Niall's neck where he'd gotten a tattoo with their initials scripted together in a circle.

Matt pulled back and started to thrust. Niall picked up his rhythm, and the cycle of pleasure overtook all awareness. Trevor's tiny gasps and Matt's deep groans mingled together. Years of loving allowed them to find the perfect position and tempo with ease. Niall's entire consciousness was consumed with his partners' presence. Each movement, each plea, their scents mingled together as the binding around their souls tightened. Trevor's shout filled the air, his ass milking Niall's cock of every drop of his essence as he poured his seed into the man he loved. Matt's roar echoed off the high ceiling, and a hot rush of fluid filled Niall's body.

They collapsed onto the bed, each of them breathing hard. Niall's heartbeat gradually slowed as he entwined his limbs with his lovers. He turned toward Matt, and their lips met, then lingered.

"Feeling better, *Caro*?"

Niall smiled. "Much." A huge yawn escaped, and he turned toward Trevor, pulling the younger man's back up against him.

"You rest. We'll let you know when dinner is ready."

Niall heard a little snore from the smaller man in front of him.

Matt chuckled. "Okay, I'll let you both know."

The bed shifted, and Niall drifted as the warmth of Trevor's body and the blanket Matt spread over them soothed him to unconsciousness.

Miranda dragged off her surgical hat and leaned against the wall of the breakroom, closing her eyes for a few blissful seconds. Her day had started at four o'clock that morning, and she'd just spent sixteen hours in surgery. The procedure had been the longest and most complicated of her career. Fortunately, Dr. Malcolm was one of the best spinal surgeons in the country, and he was optimistic that their patient would be able to walk again. The young man had a lengthy recovery and rehab ahead of him, but at least the positive prognosis made her exhausted state worth it.

She pulled out her phone and checked to see what messages had come in. The plan for the day had included Vic taking Gabriella and Charlie to school while Chase was on pick-up duty. The wallpaper on her phone was a family shot that Calleigh had taken of her children just a month or so ago. She couldn't believe how big her babies were getting. She brushed her finger gently over their delicate features, smiling at their expressions of sheer joy. Gabriella was their little blonde princess and favored Chase in looks, but Charlie shared her darker coloring. Charlie was finally settling down. They'd had a bit of a rough patch during his threes and early fours. His sassiness and general toddlerness had just about done them in. But his vivacious personality in their household was exactly what their family needed. Her phone flashed an incoming call from Vic as if she had conjured up the connection simply by thinking about him.

"Hey," she answered.

"Hello princess, I was hoping you'd be out of surgery. Everything go okay?"

"Yeah. I think so. Dr. Malcolm seems optimistic."

"So are you ready to come home?"

"God yes," she sighed. "I'm completely wasted. How are the kids?"

"Asleep. They missed you today."

Miranda closed her eyes and tried to hold back the threatening tears. "I hate not spending time with them. Thank goodness this type of surgery is rare. At least the overtime is nice."

Vic's warm chuckle reverberated through her body, waking up parts she thought were too exhausted to respond.

"I think we're doing okay without your overtime."

That was true. Her salary was far less than Vic's as current chief of radiology and Chase's income from his private practice, but it was important to her to feel as though she contributed too.

"So tonight we really need to make a decision regarding the trip. The tickets are going to have to be booked soon."

"Yeah. I'm going to clean up and change, then I'll be on my way home. Give Chase a kiss for me."

"Hmm, that's ... oh god ... yeah no problem."

"He's sucking your cock right now isn't he?"

"Uh-huh. So fucking good too."

Chase did have a bit of an oral fixation. One she'd benefited from many times over the years. She faintly heard the sounds of classical cello in the background, which was Chase's favorite music for relaxing to in the evening—which often led to less relaxing activities.

"Don't wear yourselves out, because I'm going to want some of that when I get home."

Vic groaned and cleared his throat. "Hurry home, Princess."

Chapter Four

Feburary

S he lay on the bed, her body damp with sweat and aching in all
the right places. Vic leaned down over her, and Miranda wrapped
her arms around her husband, their bodies still connected. His mouth
captured hers, and her hands linked with Chase's on Vic's back. Vic's
body bucked with each thrust of Chase's cock. Miranda tightened the
muscles of her channel, and she felt the rush of Vic's seed as he emptied
inside her. Chase tempered his groan as he came inside Vic. The hour
was early, but a little less sleep was a willing sacrifice to make to make
love to her men.

As the three of them recovered, she had a sixth sense that the rest
of the household was stirring. It had been difficult getting the kids
to sleep last night with all the excitement of their departure today.
Miranda was one part eager for the trip and two parts nervous about
all the travel with the kids. She couldn't imagine them undertaking
a vacation like this a couple of years ago, but now that Gabriella and
Charlie were a little older she was praying for a smooth operation.

"Sounds like the munchkins are awake." Chase said.

"Well, let's go intercept them before they destroy the house. I'm not leaving with the place a mess, and we have to be at the airport in just a couple of hours."

She gave Vic and Chase a quick kiss, then climbed off the bed. "I need to jump in the shower. Can one of you get their cereal ready?"

"I got it."

They all heard a crash out in the hall and groaned. Chase quickly put on a shirt and boxers. He poked his head outside their bedroom door. "Charlie! What happened?"

"I was just trying to carry my suitcase downstairs."

Miranda poked her head out below Chase's. "Sweetheart. Let your daddies do that, okay. No disasters allowed this morning."

"Okay, mom." Charlie turned to go downstairs, but stopped after one step. "Um, does that include Gabby?"

"Yes, why?"

"Well, she said she was going to make eggs for breakfast."

"Oh, fuck," Vic said behind them. "I'll get her."

"Buddy, do us a favor and go tell her that Papa is coming to take care of getting you guys' food. Tell her *not* to get the eggs out. Okay?"

Charlie shrugged. "Okay, but I no promises she'll listen to me. She never does."

Miranda closed the door and counted to five slowly while trying to hold in the giggles that usually occurred whenever Charlie opened his mouth.

"All right, you two get cleaned up while I run interference. No funny business. Get down there ASAP."

Chase saluted Vic with a smirk. "Sir, yes Sir!"

Vic pulled Chase into a hard kiss while massaging his cock through his boxers. "We'll play that game later." He pulled Miranda into his arms and buried his face against her neck. "Hmm, can never get enough of the way you smell after we love on you."

She held Vic's lips against her neck and sighed when they heard another crash from the floor below. "Go. Hurry."

Vic ran out of the room, and she heard him shout the kids' names as he hit the stairs. She looked at Chase and wrung her hands. "Please tell me this is all going to work out. I don't even care if you're lying right now."

"Honey, it's going to be fine. We're going to have a great time."

She was nervous because the group had all voted for a multi-destination trip despite her and Calleigh's initial reservations. But in the end, combining stops in Los Angeles and Oahu would make this a trip the whole family would never forget.

"Relax, you've checked and re-checked the kids' backpacks with snacks and activities for the flights. The suitcases are ready to be loaded onto the plane. They're going to go apeshit when we get to L.A. and the little excursion will give them a chance to stretch their legs and explore before we have to make our way to Oahu. Quite frankly, I can't imagine having to travel all the way across the country, then part of the Pacific without a break. It'll all be easy peasy. Trust me."

She kissed her husband and wrapped her arms around his waist. Chase was larger than Vic, with more solid muscles. She'd always felt the safest in his arms. "Your naïve optimism is exactly what I need right now." She pulled back, then headed for the en suite. "Join me? Then we'll go rescue Vic."

"Don't have to ask me twice."

As the overhead speakers announced the boarding call, everyone ran for the departure gate. Chase felt as though he were back on the football field dodging defensemen as they ran through the terminal. He kept looking over his shoulder to make sure nobody fell behind. But at the sight of six adults and five kids barreling toward them, most people at least attempted to get out of their way.

He, Vic, Miranda, Rick, Conor, and Calleigh had all come together and arranged a surprise trip to Disneyland for the kids, while the others explored the city on their own between their flights. It had been a fantastic day despite the bouts of motion sickness, lost tiaras, and consumption of way too much sugar. But they hadn't lost any of the kids! Chase had been a witness to watching the magic of Disney wash over his family, which made everything worth it. While Boston traffic had conditioned them to practicing patience, they'd learned their hometown had nothing on the nightmare that was the Los Angeles freeways.

He'd seen the absolute look of panic on Miranda's face as the minutes of traffic at a standstill crept by. Of course, it didn't help that all their phones had been blowing up with texts from the rest of the group asking them where they were. They'd budgeted a little over an hour to get back to the airport. They finally arrived at the gate, and judging by the shocked expression on the attendant's face, their group made quite the sight.

Chase pulled out his phone, which had all the boarding passes for his family. "Sorry. We're here." He pulled Vic, Miranda, and the kids up to him. "Here's our boarding passes."

"Good timing. We were about to close the doors. I believe you have some friends on board?"

Chase nodded. "Yes. We separated for the day, and getting back proved to be more complicated than expected."

The attendant looked at Charlie's shirt and Gabriella's princess dress. "I hope you had fun. Please take your seats immediately."

Miranda gasped. "Oh God, their backpacks and our carry-ons! I didn't even think about them. They're still in the lockers."

"Ma'am, I'm sorry. We really need to complete the boarding process."

"I've got them!" Rick panted as he ran up to the gate with everyone's stuff slung over his shoulders and weighing his arms down.

Miranda took their family's bags and kissed Rick's cheek. "Bless you! But how did you get the key?"

Vic helped with the kids' backpacks. "I gave it to him in the van. I knew it was going to be tight. We all took off for the gate, and he diverted to the lockers."

The group made a mad dash down the jetway. Chase saw a lone shoe that he thought belonged either to Michael or Brandon and scooped it up.

As he ducked inside the entryway to the plane he nodded to the flight attendant waiting for them. "Thank you. We're sorry we're running late."

"It's fine, Sir. Please find your seat quickly."

He scanned the cabin looking for familiar faces and spotted Ethan, Ryan and Deshawn. The three of them had visited the Aquarium of the Pacific since Deshawn loved the ocean and animals so much.

Plus, Ethan and Ryan thought the craziness of Disney might be overwhelming for the sometimes anxious boy. When they found their assigned row, Chase was immediately thankful he'd had enough miles to get the whole family upgraded to first class so the kids could recline and sleep for the six hour flight.

"Jesus, I thought you guys weren't going to make it," Clay said from the row behind them. "What happened?"

Chase held up his hand. "Just ... not now. Let me get them settled."

"Daddy, I don't feel good," Charlie moaned.

"Oh God, please not now." Chase said under his breath.

"Okay buddy. Sit down and let's buckle in." Chase saw Miranda and Gabriella across the aisle as he sat down and secured his safety restraint. "Can you tell daddy what's bothering you?"

"My head hurts."

"Okay, heads I can deal with."

Charlie was probably dehydrated from the motion sickness earlier.

"Mommy, I have to pee," Gabriella cried.

"Can you hold it till the plane takes off, sweetheart?"

Gabriella shook her head and squeezed her legs together.

Miranda took Gabby's hand, and Chase saw her and the attendant have a few words, but he looked back at Charlie.

"You're probably thirsty and I bet really tired." He looked around, but since they'd sprinted all the way from security, there was no time to fill their water bottles. A sealed bottle appeared around the edge of the seat along with Clay's smiling face. "Bless you." He took the bottle, unlocked the squeeze tip nozzle, and held it out to Charlie. "Take a drink and close your eyes. It's really late and way past your bedtime."

He peeked up over the top of the seats and saw Miranda and Gabby on their way back. There were only two seats per row on either side

of the plane, so Vic was the odd man out and comfortably settled a
couple of rows back.

I'm gonna make him pay for that one.

Gabby bounced onto the seat across from him.

"But I wanted to sit next to daddy."

"We can switch in a little while, but we really need to sit down now
because they need to take off right away. Remember, we were late, and
they were nice enough to hold the plane for us so we wouldn't miss
our trip."

Gabriella folded her arms, and a pout threatened her lips, but the
whole Disney princess look kind of ruined the effect in his opinion.
He looked over at Charlie to make sure he was doing better, but found
he was already slumped over in the seat. "Aww, little man."

He took the bottle from Charlie's slack hands and put it in the seat's
pocket. Then straightened him so his neck wasn't bent at a painful
angle. The safety video played on the screen in front of them. Chase
closed his eyes. It wasn't long before the surrounding sounds faded
out.

Clay glanced at Logan out of the corner of his eye. His husband—*how
weird and awesome is it to actually say that*—was sleeping peacefully.
There had been a time early after his discharge when a full night's sleep
had been the dream because of the PTSD. So, each peaceful night
Logan achieved was treasured. He noticed that Logan still had his

cochlear implant processors on, so Clay leaned over and kissed Logan's cheek.

"Love you," he whispered.

Logan turned toward him. Beneath his closed lids, his eyes moved quickly, indicating he was deep in dreamland. Judging by the slight smile, this dream was pleasant.

An evil little daredevil popped up on Clay's shoulder, and he glanced around the darkened cabin. Everyone around them seemed to be asleep.

He slid the blanket that had fallen between them over Logan's lap and surreptitiously searched around for his husband's zipper. Logan's hips lifted and his cock was noticeably firmer as Clay brushed his palm against it.

"What do you think you're doing?" Logan mumbled.

Clay leaned closer so his voice wouldn't carry further than their seats. "Aren't newly married couples supposed to have inappropriate displays of affection on their honeymoon?"

"We've been married for almost a year."

He sighed. "So the magic is gone." He started to take his hand away, but Logan placed his on top and pressed Clay's palm against his hard cock. Clay gave it a slight squeeze, which made Logan groan, which turned into a cough to disguise the noise.

"You're going to get us busted."

"Then let's take this somewhere a little more private. Meet me in the bathroom. Two minutes."

Logan's eyes popped open. "Seriously?"

Clay just smiled and stood up before he turned towards the center of the plane where several restrooms were located. He took a glance over his shoulder to see if Logan was watching him.

"Bow-chica-wow-wow."

Clay looked down and saw Trevor smirking as he watched some old movie with Fred Astaire on his tablet.

"You said something, Thumbelina?"

"Who me? I'm just sitting here minding my own business. Thought I might have heard some low groans coming from the row in front of me, but I'm sure it was just one of those random plane noises. Guess the noise-canceling feature on my earbuds is on the fritz."

Clay glanced at the sleeping Niall next to Trevor, then bent over so he could whisper in Trevor's ear. "I have no idea what you're talking about."

"Uh-huh. And I'm Jane Powell." He said, pointing to the screen.

"I'm not even sure how to respond to that. Now if you're finished with sophomoric taunts, then I'm going to use the restroom."

"I hope you can relieve yourself of all your tension."

Clay walked away mumbling, and he heard Trevor snicker behind him. Little brat. He slid the door to the bathroom open and glanced inside.

Just exactly how are we going to do this?

His locker at the station was bigger than this thing. Well first things first, he needed to relieve another problem.

That finished, he washed his hands and tried to turn in a complete circle, but the way the sink protruded made it obvious that double occupancy was something the engineers of this aircraft actively discouraged. He heard a tiny scratch at the door and opened it just enough to see Logan's dark head outside the door. He slid to the side as though to hide his presence from anyone.

He grabbed Logan and pulled him inside the closet-like space. Their heads collided and their feet stepped on each other. Clay got the door closed and shoved the lock in place. He pushed Logan down onto the closed toilet seat then scrambled to get his pants open again while he dragged Logan into a hard kiss that had his cock going from interested to fuck yes in two point two seconds.

"How are we ... what can...? Goddamn Clay."

"Shush. This has misdemeanor written all over it, and I am a cop."

"Then we should—"

"I said shush. Now get those pants open cause I'm going to fuck myself on your gorgeous cock, and you're going to keep me from screaming as I come."

It took Logan half a heartbeat to get with the program. Clay pulled out the sachet of lube that he'd tucked in his pocket earlier that day.

"Oh my God, you've been planning this."

He nodded. He'd followed the rules his whole life. As a cop, the law ruled his everyday existence, but for once he was going to be the moron that lived dangerously for the sole purpose of seeking a thrill. And there was nothing more thrilling than having Logan buried inside him and sending him soaring higher than this plane could ever achieve.

Logan ripped the packet from Clay's hand. He signed. *"Turn around. Hands on wall. Don't push the door."*

Clay did as instructed, his hands shaking a little. From nerves or excitement, he wasn't sure. Logan spared no time and shoved two fingers inside him. The burn with the breach made him bite his lip so hard he tasted blood, but the adrenaline racing through his body morphed any pain to pleasure. Logan's fingers disappeared, and Clay glanced in the mirror to see his husband slicking up his hard cock. He couldn't take his eyes off the sight, and when he met Logan's gaze in the mirror, the heat reflecting at him assured Clay that Logan was just as turned on by their clandestine rendezvous. Logan grabbed Clay's hips and pulled him down. He felt the crown of Logan's cock press against his hole and knew there was no going back. His need to feel Logan inside him on both a physical and emotional level far surpassed his brain's ability to think rationally. He paused for a second. Logan lifted the hand free of lube and covered Clay's mouth while he thrust up. Clay let gravity take over, allowing Logan's cock to thrust high and hard inside him.

Yes! Take me. I need all of you. All your heart. All your soul as I freely give you all of mine.

He gripped Logan's thighs, still encased in his jeans. His own were hobbled in his shorts, but all those fucking squats in the gym had to be good for something so Clay started the ride of a lifetime. Sweat beaded on his forehead as he braced his hands on either wall. Logan guided him up and down, the pace brutal and wonderful. Clay looked in the mirror. Logan's eyes were closed, his mouth open as he panted. Fear of discovery and the thrill of their illicit act had Clay on the verge of coming faster than he had ever in his life. Logan wasn't far behind, judging by how tightly his fingers dug into Clay's hips. It took everything in him to hold in the groan that threatened to erupt as his body seized with euphoria.

Clay made the sign for Logan's name and pumped his hand in the air. He ripped the paper towels off the sink he had placed there in preparation, then wrapped them around his cock as he shot volley after volley of come. He had emptied his balls, but his soul overflowed with love as Logan found his pleasure inside his body. Clay tried to catch his breath as he leaned back against Logan. His husband rubbed small circles on Clay's stomach while his cock twitched still buried inside him.

Clay stood, threw the towels away and turned on the faucet. It only took a few seconds to dampen a few more towels and give them to Logan so he could clean up. Clay leaned in so his lips were right next to Logan's processors.

"I fucking love you so much."

Logan showed Clay the sign for the same, and they shared a soft kiss.

"Now we escape."

He checked to make sure that Logan was all put back together, then flushed the toilet. Logan raised his eyebrow, but Clay just shrugged.

"We should try to make them think I was doing bathroom business."

Logan smirked and signed. *"I think the smell of sex gives it away."*

Clay pushed the handle to unlock the door. He opened the slider to find Trevor standing there.

"Hi."

Clay gave Trevor a death glare. If he even thought about saying something, his lovers were going to be down by the count of one, but to his surprise, Trevor stepped back.

"I was just keeping a lookout. You're in the clear. By the way, you'll have to teach me your technique, because had I not already suspected that you two were getting busy, I never would have suspected. I mean, seriously, when the three of us go at it, you'd think howler monkeys had invaded or something." He leaned in a little closer. "Was it worth it?"

Clay smiled. He didn't know what Logan signed behind his back, but Trevor's eyes went wide and he whistled softly.

"Bravo, gentlemen."

Chapter Five

♥

Rick walked up behind Conor and kissed the back of his neck. The room still had a dull gray early-morning hue.

"Did you sleep at all?"

"A wee bit."

Conor turned away from the hotel room window and faced Rick. He took Conor in his arms, rubbing their cheeks together, then kissed Conor's temple.

"Have I told you have much I love this beard you grew? It feels so good on my skin and makes you look incredibly hot."

Conor chuckled. "I'm glad yer loike it. It was just supposed ter keep me face warm dis winter, but it's kind of grown on me. I guess quite literally."

Conor sighed, and Rick accepted his weight. "Everything okay?"

They had arrived in Honolulu shortly after midnight. The plan for the day was for everyone to take the day to relax with their own families and get together this evening for the Paradise Cove Luau. But Rick knew Conor well enough that something was on his mind.

Conor gave Rick a quick peck, then headed to the chair in the corner, the thick cushion compressed under his weight. He glanced at

Calleigh, still asleep in their bed. The boys and Alannah were out cold in the adjoining room.

"I heard *Ar Grah'* talkin' ter Miranda de other day an' she mentioned bein' late."

Rick frowned. "Late for what? I know it was chaotic getting back to LAX after our Disney adventure."

"I think she meant late ... late."

Rick's legs went weak, and he ended up on the footrest. "Are you sure?" He did some quick math in his head, but the numbers weren't coming into focus. "Do you remember the last time she..."

Conor shook his head. "It's been so crazy wi' work, getting' ready, an' de kids' schedules. What do yer think?

Rick felt tears gather in his eyes, and he couldn't stop his lips from curving up. They'd been trying to get pregnant for almost a year.

"We're probably putting the cart before the horse here."

"What are ye batherin' aboyt?"

"What? You're not the only one who can have crazy phrases. All I'm saying is we should probably ask our wife if she actually is pregnant before we make plans or think about what colors to paint the nursery."

Conor nodded.

"I will say that I can't wait to have a ginger-haired little one with aqua eyes asking to hold us."

They had all agreed that if another baby was going to join the family, Conor should be the biological father. Since Calleigh had the boys from her first marriage and Alannah's biological parentage was pretty obvious, they wanted to make their circle complete. Not that they loved their children any differently from each other, but having a blended family that shared traits from each of them would be special.

Conor smiled. "Aye, but our wee mcnugget could end up bein' an Irish 'ellion"

Rick kneeled on the floor between Conor's legs, then ran his hands up them. He leaned in and kissed his bare stomach just above the waistband of the shamrock boxers.

"Hellion or sweet Irish rose, she or he will be part you and part Calleigh. There's no question I'll love them till the end of time."

"A chuisle mo chroí, Cáran"

"You're the pulse of my heart too."

Calleigh flipped her hair off her shoulder, but the strands just ended up back where they started as another waft of breeze coming off the ocean caressed her skin. She should have tied it up, but she knew Rick and Conor liked it when they could nuzzle her neck between the strands. She sighed and leaned back against Rick as he did exactly that. Soon they would find their seats for the dinner and show at the Paradise Cove Luau, but for the moment the group was exploring the Hawaiian village and soon the Hukilau ceremony begin.

"You doing okay, Angel?"

She nodded. "Feet hurt a little from all our walking today, but this is amazing. Thank you so much for suggesting it."

"Tell you what, when we get to the table, I'll sit across from you and give you a foot massage. You used to love that when you were pregnant with Alannah. Think it would feel nice?"

"Mmhm. And after a long day at work and on every other Sunday. Sounds like you're fishing. If you have a question, just ask me."

"Okay. You caught me. Conor thought he heard you talking to Miranda yesterday about being late and..."

"And since we've been enjoying so much practicing, you want to know if we've made it to the big game?"

"Something like that."

"I don't know yet. And that's the honest truth. Yes, I'm a couple days late, but that's happened before. I don't want to get our hopes up."

She inhaled the sweet scent of the flowers that filled the air. The petals littered the white sand of the beach beneath their feet. She held her hand up to catch an orchid as it floated towards her. Rick kissed her bare shoulder, and she heard her children's laughter. If ever she'd experienced a more dreamlike experience, she couldn't remember.

"Hey Mom?"

She looked to her right and saw Michael standing next to his brother and DeShawn. "Can we go check out the spear throwing?"

"Yes, but ask one of the other adults to go with you. I don't want you guys wandering around here alone."

"Okay!" Brandon screamed as he grabbed the other boys' hands and they ran off.

She heard the herald of the conch shell, signaling that the time had come for the fishing nets to be brought in. Many of the luau attendees headed over to watch or participate, but she wasn't interested. She scanned the immediate area looking for Alannah, and saw her and Gabriella digging in the sand near Miranda and Vic.

"What do you think our chances are of bribing the dancers to pull Niall up on stage?"

She couldn't help but laugh at the image of Mr. Introspective shaking it up on stage for hundreds to see. "I think we have a better chance of having a *Menehune* appear on stage."

"Well they do say those sneaky little buggers are nocturnal and like to party."

Soft music drifted to her on the breeze, and Calleigh saw a group of women giving a hula demonstration. Her stomach chose that moment to rumble, and Rick must have felt the vibrations because he chuckled behind her.

"Well, clearly somebody is ready for the feast that's about to begin. I think I might get myself another Mai Tai. How about you?"

She shook her head. "I'll stick with water."

Rick turned Calleigh in his arms and tilted her head up. "As soon as you're sure? Either way. We can always make a run to the drugstore. They have those here, you know."

She kissed him softly. "I know." Calleigh frowned as she spied Ryan looking at his phone and talking to Logan. It didn't seem like a cheerful conversation. "What do you suppose is going on over there?" She said, pointing behind Rick.

Rick looked over his shoulder and shrugged. "Who knows? Maybe they lost at fantasy football."

Maybe, but something seemed off to her. Both men had postures that spoke of tension and trouble. Vacation or not, some folks never quite left the office.

Ethan stared at the surfboard innocently lying on the sand. Logically he knew the thing would not jump up and bite his leg off, but that didn't mean the board didn't have nefarious intent.

"You realize I'm going to fall on my face, right?"

"Of course you are," Ryan said, smirking.

He looked up at his husband. The sun made the copper highlights in his dark hair stand out. Not something often noticeable this time of year in Boston. Especially since the forecast back home predicted the city to get another ten inches of snow today when he checked the weather app this morning.

Haha suckers!

"You don't have to look so smug about it."

Ryan squatted down and took the bar of Sex Wax away from him.

"You're doing it all wrong."

"Hey, I have exactly three hours of experience at this, and since when are you an expert surfer?"

"I wasn't always in the FBI, remember? Back when I was in the Navy, I was stationed at Pearl for a few years. I spent many hours of my misspent youth riding the pipe on the North Shore."

"Ah yes. Your rebel without a cause phase. The bad boy of the U.S. Navy. I'm still surprised the Feds let you join their black-suit party."

Ryan put the bar of wax down. "Don't forget I know all your dirty little secrets you keep hidden behind that straight-laced lawyer façade."

Ethan quickly looked over his shoulder. "Shush. Deshawn doesn't need to know that we were anything other than the responsible adults he's familiar with."

Ryan chuckled and shook his head. "Right," he said slowly. "Okay, you're all set. Remember what the instructor said yesterday?"

"Umm. Sort of. Paddle, float, stand, surf. Nothing to it!"

"Oh man, this is going to be good. Hey D, are you ready to show your dad up on the waves?"

"Yeah! Try not to get eaten by a shark, Dad."

Ethan shook his head. "Well, if I see one, I'll just tell him that younger boys have more tender meat. I'm all tough and grisly."

Ryan felt around his shorts, then took his phone out of his pocket. He looked down and frowned.

"What's wrong?" Ethan asked.

"Nothing. Just work stuff."

"Ry, we're on vacation."

"Baby, there's no such thing as a vacation for the guy in charge. It just means I'm out of the office. But don't worry; it's nothing urgent. Just another notice from Washington regarding some chatter."

"About what?"

Ryan looked at Ethan, but didn't say anything.

"Right. Need to know. Well, do me a favor. If that chatter says some nutcase plans on setting off a nuke in Pearl City, you'll let me know, right?"

"Baby, if that were to happen, it wouldn't matter if I told you or not. We'd all be dead anyway."

"Not if the 5-0 Task Force was on the case. They prevent terrorist attacks on a weekly basis. And they do it in spectacular style."

"You're obsessed with that show. It's been out of syndication for years."

"Alex O'Loughlin is hot. And I never watched it when it was on, so now I get to binge the entire series!"

"I won't argue with your assessment of Alex's attractiveness. However, you realize how unrealistic those storylines are, right? I mean, Navy Seal or not, nobody can save the world that many times."

"Aww, don't worry, I don't need Alex when I have my very own superhero."

Ethan wrapped his arms around Ryan's waist and kissed him.

"Dad, stop sucking face and let's go!"

"As much as I would love to make out with you in the sand, our son is currently diving through the break waves."

Ethan spun around. "Deshawn Harrison-Ashton stop right there!" He picked up the surfboard and high-kneed his way into the surf.

Ryan kept his eye on the water where the two men who owned his heart were paddling out toward the waves side by side. He unlocked his phone and hit a button, connecting him to the number that had left the text message a few minutes ago.

"Talk to me."

"Sorry to interrupt your vacation, but we have something that might be actionable in your area."

"Then call the Honolulu office."

"We did, and they're expecting you. We just received confirmation that Shin Kyung made his way through customs at the Honolulu airport under one of his aliases twelve days ago."

"Are you fucking with me? You're telling me that the man responsible for the attempted assassination of the South Korean president less than a year ago just fucking flew into Hawaii for a goddamn vacation!"

"There's more."

"Of course there is."

"Yesterday we detained and interrogated an individual on a separate matter. However, during the course of the interrogation, he revealed he had ties to the break-in of the Lincoln Stoddard Army Reserve Center in Worchester last year. We convinced him it was in his best interest to reveal what happened to the stolen weapons."

"Let me guess. They sold them."

"Yep, to the NPA. And their contact was..."

"Kyung?"

"No. He'd wouldn't allow that kind of exposure, but after some fast clicking fingers in the known associates' database, we uncovered a link to him. Ryan, our guy said that they got their hands on the three M1A1 launchers and a stockpile of rockets."

"Those things could be anywhere by now. No reason to think he brought them here."

"True. But, I know you spent hours arguing with the Governor that there was more to that break-in than the lone idiot after a cache of handguns and assault rifles. Here's your validation."

Ryan waved at Ethan and Deshawn, who were bobbing on the surface of the ocean. Blissfully ignorant of a terrorist who was on the same island as them. As long as it was in his power to do so, it would remain that way.

"All right, I'll contact the special agent in charge here. For all we know, this was just a jumping point for Kyung. He could have already crawled into a hole elsewhere."

"What's your gut say?"

Ryan sighed. "Nothing good. What does he have to gain from popping his head up here and now when he's been untraceable for the last decade? Look, I've got to go."

"Try not to get sunburned."

"You mean of the nuclear variety?"

"Especially that kind."

He hung up the phone just as Ethan and Deshawn caught a wave. "That's my boys, woohoo!"

Trevor stopped walking and took a drink from his water bottle. He adjusted the straps of his backpack and absorbed the jungle scents around him. He, Matt and Niall had hired a local guide to help them navigate their way up to the ridge known as K2. One of the two peaks on *Pu'u Konahuanui*, part of the Koolau mountain range on the east side of O'hau. So far, the paths were well maintained and graded, but it was a good thing Holokai acted as their navigator because they had wound their way through three different trails so far. Holokai swore it was just a little further before they left the jungle for the openness of the ridgeline.

"You okay, *Bello*?" Matt asked.

"Fine. Just taking it all in. Look at those roots. It looks like a sea of snakes covering the ground."

Matt gave a shudder, and Trevor wrapped his arm around his lover's waist. "Don't worry, I'll protect you."

"This coming from the man who shrieked at the sight of the crayfish in the river last summer when we hiked that trail in Washington?"

"Hey, those things are nasty! All beady-eyed with tentacles that just feel their way around till they can pinch you with their little circus claws."

"Sure. Come on, let's go. Niall and Holokai have disappeared around the bend and I don't know about you, but I don't want to get lost in here. One wrong turn and we might end up in a Yakuza drug stash or maybe even come across some kind of airshaft that leads to a secret underground military base."

"And you say I have a crazy imagination?"

They carefully made their way across the uneven ground. Trevor thought he heard a noise off to his right, but when he looked there was nothing there. Of course, he couldn't see more than a couple of feet into the foliage. He squinted and thought he saw a dark shadow of movement.

Great, now Matt has me jumping at shadows.

Trevor pushed his way through bushes that slapped at his shins like hundreds of vicious little guards.

Good thing I listened to Holokai and attached the lower portion of my convertible pants.

They broke through, and he looked out across the valley. He also saw that what had been an easy stroll through the jungle was about to get much more difficult.

Can humans walk that vertical?

The path, and that was a generous term, narrowed to the point that it was little more than a dirt rut. In fact, when he looked ahead, it appeared as though Niall and Holokai were perched on the side of the mountain with nothing but a sheer cliff below them. He swallowed hard and made his way up to where the others stood.

"You see now why I chose this trek?" Niall asked when they met them.

Trevor nodded. "You've just confirmed what I suspected years ago. You're freaking nuts! One misplaced foot and you and Matt get to inherit my classic movie collection."

Niall took Trevor's hand and slowly turned him. He wrapped his arms around Trevor's waist and pulled him close. "Close your eyes, count to five, and when you open them tell me again what you see."

Trevor leaned back, trusting Niall to keep him safe. He did as asked and gasped as he looked out across the valley. Jagged green peaks pierced the pale blue sky. A light breeze brought him the scents of earth and flowers. Trevor almost thought he could even smell the clouds as they moved in from the coast. His gaze followed the ridges and peaks that had terrified him a moment ago, only now his feet itched to race to the top just so he could proclaim his conquering success.

"Now do you understand?"

He tilted his head back, silently begging for Niall's kiss. "Yes."

They continued making their way up the mountain. Trevor had to be careful about his footing in many places, because rain had eroded the path. His heart raced as they made their way up a big ol' butt hill.

Damn, *it's a good thing we run every morning.*

Holokai stopped when they reached a flat overlook area, and Trevor was glad for another break. He'd come a long way from his days of hibernating in the tiny Dorchester apartment he'd called home before moving in with Matt and Niall, but this was clearly a hike intended for experienced climbers.

When Niall had suggested it, Trevor had had his worries about their readiness, but Niall had turned to him and explained that this excursion gave him the chance to commune with the native spirits and deities of the islands. His lover may be Mohegan, but he shared an affinity with the natives of all the regions they had explored on their travels. The rest of Trevor's objections had fallen silent.

Niall looked at Holokai and asked, "Do these mountains hold a sacred place for your people and culture still?"

"Unfortunately, as the older generations begin their journey to *Lua-o-Milu*, land of the spirits, many of the beliefs of our ancestors are lost. I suspect the same can be said of your people," Holokai said.

Niall nodded.

"I remember being a small boy and sitting beside my *tutu*. She used to say nature and our people are one and the same. The land, water, ocean, and sky were the very foundations of life, and the embodiments of the gods and deities. Respect and care for nature, in turn means that nature will care for us."

"In some ways, my people shared similar views. One of our oldest stories speaks of the *Makiawisug*, or Little People. After nightfall, the call of the Whip-poor-will signals their arrival. The *Makiawisug* must be treated with respect. Offerings of food, like corn and berries or even meat, were left in baskets throughout the wood. In return for this kindness, they kept the earth well and taught our people how to cultivate the land and use healing plants."

Trevor laid his hand on Niall's back. "Thousands of miles and hundreds of generations may have separated your people from Holokai's but it sounds like they may have gotten along."

Trevor looked up. The peak of the mountain loomed high above his head. Maybe there was something sacred about this mountain, maybe not. But it was intense and awe-inspiring. They'd made it about halfway up, but the next section looked pretty vertical. The sky had grown overcast, and the air humid. His T-shirt stuck to his chest. He followed Niall and Holokai with Matt bringing up the rear. Partway up, Trevor made the mistake of looking over the edge. It had to be over two thousand feet down, and the trail they were walking on was maybe two feet wide, very overgrown, and littered with deep ruts from erosion.

"Just keep looking forward, *Bello*." Matt said.

Trevor nodded. *Who knew I'm afraid of heights?*

The last section to the top had ropes anchored into the mountain. He pulled himself up. When he got to the top, the entire city of Honolulu stretched out on one side of him and the Pacific on the other.

"Wow," he whispered.

Niall took out one of his cameras and started shooting. Trevor caught his breath and looked down at where they'd come from. This was his first real mountain hike, so to speak, and damned if he didn't love it. Now that it was over.

"Hey Matt, are we going back the same way?" he asked.

"No." Matt snuggled up behind him and pointed in the direction opposite to where they'd come from. "See that peak over there?"

Trevor's gaze followed across a crazy ass thin ridge with literally nothing but sheer drops on either side to the peak Matt pointed to.

"I should have known."

"I've got your back, and it looks worse than it really is."

Why don't I believe him?

It wasn't very long before Niall packed away his cameras. These must have been memoir photos because had his partner been working, the photo shoot would have lasted much longer as he waited for just the right light and switched out to a few different lenses. They got packed up and prepared to go on. He took a few steps, but then stopped.

"Niall?"

Niall turned and faced Trevor. He watched his lover's black hair sway with the wind. Despite the trappings of a modern man, Trevor saw the soul beneath. He saw the echo of Niall's heritage. All the warriors who had lived, fought, and loved. And he understood.

"Thank you for letting me share this with you."

Niall walked towards him. "I share my soul with you. Wherever I am, so are you. In this time, the previous and the next."

Hearing these types of words from his lover still made him catch his breath and his heart skip a beat. For someone who had felt alone most of his life, it was simultaneously comforting and terrifying to accept Niall's pledge.

Matt closed the gap behind him, and Trevor found himself held securely between his men on the edge of a mountain with only the sky and the earth to serve as witnesses.

"I love you both with everything that I am. That is all I have to give."

Matt kissed the back of Trevor's neck. "And that is the greatest gift on earth."

They continued on their trek. Trevor noticed that Holokai was some distance ahead, as if he'd sensed their need for privacy. The windward side of the mountain range looked like green bedsheets with ripples that fell to the jungle floor beneath them. He kept stopping to look around, mesmerized by the views and nature surrounding him.

Niall stopped suddenly. "Down!"

One second Trevor was spying on the peak where they headed, and the next he watched as Holokai's head snap back. A couple of seconds later Holokai dropped off the edge of the mountain. Trevor blinked, not sure exactly what he was seeing. Then, a warrior's cry filled the air, and Niall disappeared over the edge of the trail.

"Niall!" Trevor screamed.

"Trevor, get down!" Matt yelled.

He found himself yanked to the ground. The binoculars he'd been holding flew from his hands. He tasted dirt, branches scratched his arms and rocks dug into his knees, but all he noticed was the blood splattering across the leaves of the brush where Niall had disappeared. All he could see was Niall's foot, which was too still. He scrambled in Niall's direction. The leaves in front of him exploded.

"Stop, *Bello*! Don't give him something to aim at."

"What are you talking about? Let me go! We have to help him."

"We can't."

Trevor couldn't see through the tears. His throat burns from the screams. "Don't say that!"

Matt crawled and gathered Trevor into the circle of his arms, practically laying on top of him. "Listen to me. I will not let you make yourself another target. I don't know if we've lost Niall, but I will damn sure make it so that I don't lose you. Someone is up there on that ridge with a sniper rifle."

He clung to Matt as leaves exploded around them. His tears of agony mixed with sweat born of terror. Matt grunted and his body jerked.

"Matt?"

"I'm okay. Just grazed me. I think the brush is making it hard for the shooter to see us down here on the ground."

Silence filled the air for several heartbeats. Trevor opened his eyes only to see the gray cotton of Matt's T-shirt. He tried to peer over his shoulder, but Matt had him effectively pinned down. Trevor sucked in a breath as Matt levered himself up.

"They stopped." Matt said. "Don't stand up. Keep low to the ground in case they're waiting us out."

Trevor scrambled to where Niall had fallen

"I don't know if he's breathing!"

There was a lot of blood. Too much blood. It was spreading across Niall's chest and turning his white shirt a horror-inducing crimson. His vision swam, and static noise filled his ears.

People check for pulses, right?

He stuck his fingers on Niall's neck. Nothing. Was he not doing it right, or was there nothing there?

Please, *Manto or Milu or whatever God may exist out there. Help me. Let me know if he's still alive.*

Matt grabbed Trevor's hands and stopped his agitated movements. "I can't get a signal on my phone."

Trevor turned to face Matt. His handsome face was a mask of pain and disbelief. "Did I see...? Holokai, it looked like ... I saw him fall up the trail and I ... I think they shot him ... in the head."

Only then did he spot the blood on Matt's biceps.

"Oh, fuck, he got you too!"

Trevor tried to shove Matt's sleeve up to see the damage. He swallowed down the bile that tried to rise. Sure, he worked for the police department, but it's not like he was a real cop. He was a lab rat, for fuck's sake. He didn't have any actual experience in emergency situations. And it wasn't as if he remembered the lessons from the basic three-hour first aid class all techs took every couple of years. This is what 911 was for! Matt took hold of Trevor's fingers and held them. He looked up and noticed that Matt wasn't even breathing fast, unlike himself, who was two heartbeats away from hyperventilating.

"I'm okay. I promise. Niall?" Matt choked out.

"I don't know."

Chapter Six

♥

Ryan stepped into the lobby of the FBI headquarters in Honolulu. The recent construction showcased an impressive spectacle. Four stories with lots of glass, smaller than his home base in Chelsea, but similar in design. He'd stopped by the hotel room for a quick change. Thankfully, he packed a suit for the dinner at *Azure* the adults had planned later that week. His shirt was a deep purple, and there was no tie, but he figured it was better than showing up in his beachwear. He showed the guard his badge before walking through the metal detectors.

This is something I didn't plan on doing on my vacation.

"Can you please direct me to Agent Delgado's office?" He asked the guard.

"Yes, Sir. Take the elevator to the fourth floor. His office is four-two-one."

"Thank you."

Ryan followed the guard's directions with ease. He was looking up and down the hall for the right office door, figuring the special agent in charge of the field office earned himself a proper office as opposed to the cubicles scattered around. He turned and came face to face with a rather constipated-looking man.

"Can I help you with something, mister?"

Ryan shook his head and tried to move past the man. "No, I'm fine, thank you."

"You don't have a visitor's pass. I'm going to need to see some ID."

We're going to play this game? So glad I canceled my afternoon of snorkeling for this.

He pulled out his badge folio and showed it to Mr. Congeniality.

The agent gave Ryan a long look. "Not exactly Bureau dress."

"I'm on vacation. You're lucky I didn't show up in board shorts and flip-flops. Now I'm here to see Delgado. I believe he's expecting me."

"Is he? And exactly why is a tourist from Boston meeting with the agent in charge?"

He'd had enough of Agent Asshole on a power trip. "Look, I was called here to consult on an active investigation. I'm happy to help in any way I can, but I would like to get back to my family at some point this afternoon."

The agent snorted and smiled. "Let me guess. We interrupted your plans of watching nearly naked women walk up and down Waikiki Beach from behind your sunglasses while your wife sucks down pina coladas from the amazingly attractive pool boys at alarming rates?"

"Fuck this." Ryan brought out his phone and hit the last logged number. "Hey, Steven? I'm standing somewhere outside your office. Will you open your damn door?" Ryan listened for a moment and smiled. "Why yes, as a matter of fact, I believe so." He winked at agent asshole. "Really? I'll be sure to pass on the message."

He disconnected the call and slipped the phone back into his pocket. "Umm, so thank you very much for the warm welcome. I really see what the islanders mean by the spirit of Aloha." He pushed his way past toward an office whose door now stood open. He turned to look over his shoulder. "Oh, and Special Agent Delgado has informed me you'll be sitting in on our meeting. Would you mind running down to the cafeteria and grabbing us a couple of coffees? I take mine black with one cream. I'm sure you already know how your boss takes his, since you get several each day."

Ryan saw the man's face turn an alarming shade of red. Clearly he was about to explode, most likely all over Ryan. But then, behind Ryan came the sound of someone clearing their throat.

"I think I'd like a bear claw too, Patterson."

Ryan nearly lost it, but refused to look away from the junior agent who served as Steven's assistant.

"Yes, Sir. Anything else?"

"No. Ryan, come on in and make yourself comfortable. Agent Noelani Mahi'ai should be here momentarily. She's the one who discovered the intel."

Ryan turned his back on Patterson and entered Steven's office. Once the door was closed, he looked at his friend and chuckled. "Holy shit. Do you test the coffee for arsenic before drinking it?"

"Hell, I don't drink that shit. I just make him go get it when he gets particularly high-handed. The guy has bounced from department to department because of his attitude. Unfortunately, we can't kick him out of the Bureau for being a douche."

Ryan sat down in the chair. "So how did you end up with him?"

"Because I can ignore him. And send him on pointless errands when he gets to be too insufferable. So how are Ethan and Deshawn?"

Ryan smiled. "They're fantastic. Went surfing this morning, Deshawn is on his way to the water park with some of our friends, and tonight we're doing some kind of sunset paddle boarding adventure on the Heleiwa River. I'm looking forward to seeing the sea turtles."

"Ethan ... went surfing?"

"Mm-hm."

"How did that go?"

"About what you would expect. He's got a new nickname."

Steven smile. "Do I want to know?"

"Sharkbait. Deshawn was joking with him before they went out that Ethan was so slow he'd be a good snack, then they actually saw what they claimed to be a fin sticking up from the water before their last ride. Needless to say, they didn't go back out."

"It happens. There are usually close to a dozen incidents each year with the various species. Look, I'd love to sit here and shoot the shit, but there was a reason your vacation got interrupted."

"Right. Shin Kyung."

Someone rapped on the door. Agents Patterson and Mahi'ai came in. Patterson with the coffee and one donut. He had an expression that was such the antithesis of his previous that either the man had mainlined some Xanax or he had the type of control that Ryan had only seen during interrogation. Bluster and bullshit he dealt with every day. But a calculated sociopath was a whole other ballgame.

"Great, now we can get started. Let's bring Agent Ashton up to speed with what we have, then he can tell us what he knows about Kyung."

"Mr. Ashton, it's an honor to meet you," Noleani said.

"Thank you. You as well. Agent Delgado's told me good things about you. Please call me Ryan." He turned to accept the suspiciously tepid cup of coffee from Patterson. "Thanks." Ryan turned back to face Steven and set the cup on his desk. "So do we know how Kyung got through customs without being flagged in the first place?"

"Yes, Sir, he was using a US Passport with the identity of a Hawaiian resident. A Mr. Sung Min."

"Just out of curiosity, is there a Mr. Sung Min?"

"Why would you want to know that?" Patterson asked with a sneer.

Ryan turned and studied the man for a few seconds before he answered. No sweat beading, pulse steady, and his gaze met him with a hint of suspicion in their green depths.

"Because I'd like to know if there's a dead body we need to search for."

The silence hung in the air until Steven cleared his throat. "No such name exists in any records that we've found. Looks like it was just a fake."

"So what raised the red flag?" Ryan asked.

Noelani removed a photo from a file folder she held. "One of the TSA officers recognized Kyung on the monitors. He apparently checks our most wanted lists regularly. Unfortunately, by the time he verified the connection, Kyung had left the terminal."

Ryan took a moment to study the photo. It wasn't a quality shot because Kyung was clearly trying to be inconspicuous, although he hadn't taken great pains to change his appearance that much. Shin Kyung was an American citizen. Born and raised in Palisades Park, New Jersey until the age of twelve, when his father was transferred back to South Korea for his job with Hanjin Shipping. He was extremely intelligent, extremely well educated and extremely hateful of all things western.

"So we know the how. What about the why?"

Steven leaned forward and braced his arms on his desk. "That is why we called you. You know this man probably better than anyone else in the bureau."

Patterson snorted under his breath and tried to cover it up with a sneeze. "Sorry. Must be dusty in here. What makes him such an expert?"

He'd had just about enough of this shithead. Having put in over twenty years with the FBI, he didn't need to justify himself to some trumped-up Cub Scout. Not to say he got along or agreed with all his colleagues, but there was a healthy respect among his peers for their respective abilities.

"How about the fact that Agent Ashton received the Director's Leadership Award when he graduated from Quantico. He spent five years assigned to the organized crime unit in New York. His reserve unit was called up for deployment where he served on the U.S.S John F Kennedy during Operation Enduring Freedom. Afterward, he came back and received a promotion to supervisory special agent in Boston's Counterintelligence office. He transferred to the Special Security Branch-Terrorism unit where he managed the international terrorism task force for twelve years. Then just a year ago became the Special Agent in Charge of the Boston division. Word on the street is he's headed toward becoming an executive assistant director in the next five years."

"Jesus, you have notes from my entire professional career in that folder, Mahi'ai?"

"No, Sir. I neglected to pull your transcripts from either your Bachelor's or Law degrees from the University of Pittsburgh. And please call me Noelani."

"I'm not sure if I should be impressed with your thoroughness or report you for stalking."

Steven stood and walked over to the window. "Bottom line is, Ryan is as close to an expert on Shin Kyung as we have. We're lucky he just happened to be here on the island, and was professional enough to interrupt his family vacation to help us. So if you don't start treating him with respect, then you'll be mopping the floors instead of getting us coffee." He turned to face Patterson. "Got it?"

"Yes, Sir."

"Good. Now can we please figure out what this fucker is doing on my island?"

Ryan stood and paced Steven's office. He always thought better when he was moving. "I received a call from Boston earlier regarding a link between Kyung and some stolen weapons I was investigating last year. Now, personally, I think those weapons are long gone, but we can't afford not to consider the possibility."

"What kind of weapons are we talking about?"

"Military grade. A few M1A1 rocket launchers and a cache of small arms."

"Bazookas? While they can create havoc, I don't think Kyung is going to take over Hawaii with them. He's more of a subversive attacker. Just look at his attempt on the South Korean president. He tried to release saran gas through the HVAC system of the Blue House."

Noelani nodded. "True, but we also suspect he was responsible for the car bomb in Stockholm just a few months ago. That shows a level of escalation. What if his next attack is something like a dirty bomb? Getting access to materials wouldn't be difficult, and quite frankly, who's to say Kyung doesn't hire out his services? North Korea has certainly been doing a lot of posturing lately. Getting an American citizen to do their dirty work would be quite a coup for them."

"What if he's not planning anything at all? What if he really came here for vacation?" Patterson asked.

Everyone in the room turned toward him. Fortunately, Ryan had a good view from the back of the room. If Steven's eyebrows got any closer together, he might need a crowbar to pry them apart, and Noelani was in danger of catching flies; her mouth was open so wide.

Steven pinched the bridge of his nose and let out a long breath. "While I will concede there is probably a one in a billion chance that might be the case, it is our job to be three steps ahead of guys like

Kyung so we can be proactive instead of reactive. Our job is to prevent the shit from hitting the fan so that the people of Hawaii aren't even aware there are numerous threats to their safety on a weekly basis."

"I think we could all use a refill." Patterson said and left the room.

"Thank fuck," Ryan said under his breath.

He heard Steven and Noelani snicker softly.

"Alright, in my experience, there are a few key areas to a successful terrorist plot. Money to fund it, strategy to make sure it goes off as planned, technology to be current with arms and methods of control, media to make sure people see it, fundamentalists to take credit for it, and the power players who gain the most benefit from it. As you said, this is your island. So if Kyung is going to pull something off, let's talk this out and figure out how?"

The boat rocked under his feet, and Logan leaned against the rail. He still had some balance issues once in a blue moon, and the rail made him feel more secure.

"This is so cool!" Clay yelled into the wind as they rode the waves in search of humpback whales.

He glanced over at his husband and smiled. Clay had been bouncing around all day. It was fun to see a man who normally shouldered way too much adult stress act like a little kid. So far, this whole honeymoon had been everything Logan could have wished for. All except for that niggling feeling at the back of his neck.

Clay turned to face Logan and signed. *"Are you having fun?"*

"Yes. Always wanted to do this."

They were using sign because the background noise from the boat and wind prevented him from hearing any speech clearly.

"Me too. I know we have boats in Boston, but there's always so much to do."

"I know. And this is Hawaii. It's a new level of fun. Hey, what were you talking to Ryan about at the Luau? It seemed way too serious for a Honeymoon."

"You know that feeling you get when there's something itchy on the back of your neck?"

"Sure. It's saved my life a few times."

Logan nodded. Back when he was a soldier, he'd learned never to ignore that tiny voice in his head. However, despite years of therapy for the PTSD, he still felt robbed of the ability to trust that feeling when it came upon him.

"I had it all last night at the Luau and I wanted to talk with Ryan because I thought maybe I was just imagining things. You know?"

Clay put his hand on Logan's shoulder. "I hear you," he voiced. "What did Ryan say?"

"He said he would keep his eyes and ears open, but there was no imminent threat as far as he knew. But it's still there, like a phantom blowing a waft of rancid breath across my skin."

"Just because Ryan didn't confirm your suspicions, doesn't mean they're not valid. I will always trust you. I trust you with my family. I trust you with my life. I trust you with my heart."

"I love you, Clayton Phillips."

"And I love you. Now let's watch some whales blow each other."

He put his arm around his husband and shook his head. "Pervert."

Chapter Seven

♥

M att stopped and looked behind him down at the makeshift litter he and Trevor had put together from tree branches and large plants. "Let's rest for a few minutes."

"No! We have to keep going. We have to get him to the hospital." Trevor said.

"*Bello*, he has a sucking chest wound. I need to ensure that our bandage is still holding tight. By keeping the hole covered, we can prevent air from moving in and out of the chest cavity. He needs the air to get into his good lung so we can keep circulation going. It's the best thing we can do to save his life until we get help."

"Oh yeah. That's good. Sorry. Sorry. I'm just..."

Matt walked around the litter that held their unconscious lover and took Trevor into his arms. "I'm scared too. But he's a strong man. And we're more than halfway down the mountain. We should be in phone reception soon, and then we'll get him some help from someone who practices emergency medicine."

They kneeled next to Niall. It had been many years since Matt had done ER rotations during medical school, but he still remembered the basics. Trevor brushed Niall's hair off his forehead, and Matt took Niall's pulse. It was rapid, which indicated his heart was working faster to maintain circulation. The bullet had gone all the way through Niall's chest. The exit wound was jagged. They'd fashioned a bandage from a sandwich bag and extra shirt Trevor had in his backpack. What worried Matt the most was how much blood was leaking into Niall's chest, because that would put pressure around the heart and lungs, affecting his blood pressure.

"We're almost there, Niall. Just hang on for us," Trevor whispered.

Matt bent over and kissed Niall. He thought he might have heard a barely audible groan, so he did it again. This time there was a definite sound.

Trevor gasped. "Niall? Wake-up. Can you open your eyes?"

Their lover's eyes fluttered but didn't open. Matt looked over at Trevor, whose blue eyes held so many questions, but now also a flicker of hope. He cupped Trevor's face and brought their lips together. Kissing Trevor was like sitting in front of a roaring fire, eating ice cream, and making stuff blow-up all at once. If Niall was the foundation for their home, Trevor was the mortar that held them together.

He pulled away from Trevor's lips and looked down to find they were each holding one of Niall's hands. "Let's get our man down this mountain."

Calleigh took a deep breath and let it out slowly. She stared at herself in the bathroom mirror and smiled. "Guess there's no going back now."

She opened the door and found Rick and Conor sitting next to each other on the bed. They leaned forward, gripping each other's hands. Conor's jaw dropped a little, and Calleigh couldn't help but preen a little. Thirty-three, three kids and she could still turn her husbands' heads.

"Holy shoite *Mo Ghrá*, yer a *beure*. Now get over 'ere so we can strip yer bare an' love on yer for donkey's years."

Calleigh giggled. She couldn't help it. A little over ten years since she'd met her men, and Conor's way with words still could make her both hot and laugh simultaneously.

"Where in the world did you get that little scrap of fabric angel?" Rick asked.

Calleigh tried to strike a pose in the frame of the bathroom door. "Miranda and I went shopping. I thought since we earned an afternoon without the kids we should make the most of it."

"Oh my, we owe Miranda, Chase, and Vic an enormous favor." Rick said.

Calleigh laughed. "They're calling it in tomorrow."

"Then let's not waste their generous gift. Come 'ere *Ar Ghrá.*"

Calleigh made her way toward the bed. "The two of you are wearing way too many clothes. Rick, I want you to get Conor nice and hard."

"My pleasure." Rick said as he turned to strip Conor's shirt off.

"With your mouth." She said.

Rick grinned, and Conor moaned. She watched Rick slide his hands up Conor's chest. Rick's darker complexion stood out against Conor's pale skin. Their mouths met in a kiss that made Calleigh's heart race. Rick pushed Conor back on the bed then used his mouth to the best advantage, encouraging Conor to arch his neck with each caress. They stripped each other, and Rick made his way down between Conor's legs. Calleigh could practically taste Conor's flesh as Rick licked up their husband's hard cock.

She moved to the side of the bed for a better view. Conor turned his head and opened his eyes. The aquamarine color reflected so much love that Calleigh found herself tearing up. She'd been a bit of a watering pot lately.

"I almost didn't even want ter take that off yer."

She'd given into Miranda's suggestion that she get the super sexy green negligee. The shiny satin chemise dress hugged every one of her curves, including a few that hadn't been there a couple of years ago. Wired cups molded to her breasts, which nearly spilled over the top.

She slid the dress up a little to give Conor a view underneath the hem. "Well, technically you don't have to."

"Ah feck. Brin' dat juicy wee tin' over 'ere."

Calleigh climbed onto the bed and kneeled over Conor's face. That wicked Irish tongue was good at more than talking. Rick gave the head of Conor's cock one last lick then moved up his body. Calleigh reached out, and Rick took her into his arms. Conor groaned, and the vibrations resonated through her. She moaned into Rick's mouth.

Conor held her hips, and she poised herself above him. His tongue flicked and lapped at her core with a dexterity that had her writhing, moaning and using Rick as a lifeline. Rick cupped her breast and thumbed the hard, satin covered, nipple. He manipulated each tip till they ached so much the silky fabric became torturous. Rick's finger dipped between her folds to play with her clit, rubbing back and forth, stimulating the bundle of nerves. Conor's tongue speared inside her, and she jerked so hard she nearly lost her balance. Rick's tongue flicked against her breasts in the same rhythm his finger slowly played her hungry flesh.

"Please," she begged.

Her men were driving her insane with need. Calleigh craved a much deeper touch. She wanted to feel them inside her.

"Yer needin' *Ar Ghrá* ?"

"Mmhm." She nodded and tried to get Rick's touch deeper.

"We've got you, Angel."

Calleigh moaned as two fingers pushed inside her. Slowly, they stretched her. She knew Conor's cock must be hard and leaking, but she couldn't see it behind Rick, who straddled Conor's waist. She could, however, see that Rick's erection deserved some attention. Calleigh took him in hand and stroked the hard flesh, till a bead of fluid formed on the tip. Calleigh slid her thumb across the slit and smeared the drop of pre-cum around the sensitive cap.

"Angel, you're playing with fire down there."

"I know. I'm stoking it to make sure it's nice and hot."

Rick growled and pulled his fingers out of Calleigh's pussy. She gasped when he lifted her off Conor and flipped her around. Calleigh ended up straddling Conor's hips. She ground herself against his cock and watched Conor arch his head back and clutch the sheets until his biceps bulged.

"You're going to ride him, Angel. And then I'm going to slide my cock in your pretty little ass."

"Oh yes, I can't wait to have you shove your dick deep inside me, but first I want to watch Conor slick up your cock for me."

"Feck, I love it when yer got a derdy wee gob."

Calleigh snickered. She enjoyed shocking Rick and Conor with her naughty girl persona. She picked up the lube from the mattress.

"Rick get to where Conor can wrap his hand around your cock."

Rick shuffled to the side of them. "Put your hand out, Conor." Calleigh put a dollop of lubrication in Conor's hand. She tossed the tube back on the bed, then slid her hand up Rick's abs, tweaking a hard nipple along the way until she wrapped her arm around his neck. She stared into the sapphire eyes that matched her daughter's. "Now slick up his cock so it slides in real nice and easy." Rick closed his eyes and moaned. He hissed, and his fingers dug into Calleigh's hips. "Good. Now slide those slick fingers into my ass and stretch me open."

"Oh God, Angel. You're killing me."

She scooted up, so she was within Conor's reach. She braced her hands on his chest while he first circled her entrance, then she let out a groan when he breached the tight muscle. Conor stretched her until he had three fingers moving within her. Calleigh road his fingers, moaning while gripping Rick's arms and bracing her forehead on his shoulder.

"Gran', *muirnín*. Yer are ready."

She shifted around and perched above Conor's long cock. While staring into her husband's eyes, Calleigh slowly sank down, taking him within her aching body. Once their groins were flush, she sighed. She rose to her knees, and when just the tip of Conor's cock remained inside her, she slowly lowered herself down again. Her body demanded a fiercer possession. She rose, then let her weight carry her down harder, tilting her hips so Conor reached the deepest part of her. Her fingertips dug into Conor's chest as she moved up and down. Closing her eyes, she concentrated on sensations.

Rick took hold of Calleigh's hips and stopped her. She let out a little growl, but then he pushed her forward to lie against Conor. Conor wrapped his arms around her and held her open for Rick. She felt the head of his cock poised at her opening, and he pushed forward.

"Fuck you feel so good, Angel," Rick said as the head of his cock popped through the ring of muscle.

He worked his entire length in. Calleigh panted against Conor's neck the entire time.

"*Gu sealladh saelbh oirnn.*" Conor whispered.

Calleigh loved it when he spoke Irish. That phrase being one that she'd finally learned. It roughly meant 'heaven preserve my sanity because she owns my soul'. But she had every intention of destroying his sanity while they took each other to heaven. Conor and Rick moved.

"I can feel yer *Càran. Ár ghrá* 'olds us inside 'er perfectly."

"Aye. She's hot, tight, and my cock fits inside her little ass just right."

"Mmhm, an' next time it's gonna be in me."

Calleigh really hoped there wasn't a family staying next door because their moans echoed in the room. She rode the edge of her orgasm as her heart filled with love amidst each thrust of Rick and Conor's cocks in and out of her body. The three of them transferred sloppy kisses back and forth. Rick's and Conor's firm fingers traced lines of ecstasy across her body. Intense pleasure rippled through her, layering itself upon the love she held in her heart for her husbands.

Conor slipped his fingers between his and Calleigh's bodies. His fingertip found her clit and rubbed it in tiny circles. Calleigh couldn't hold in the cry as tiny fireworks radiated across all her nerve endings from the extra stimulation. He and Rick thrust hard inside her. Rick plunged deep and held still. Calleigh's pussy clamped down as the tension inside her exploded into starbursts of pleasure. Conor's cry of completion came just as Calleigh felt his release find home deep inside her.

Long minutes later, when their breathing evened out, they separated their frames and tucked Calleigh between them. Hands and lips crisscrossed and soothed their sensitized skin. The windows and sliding door to their room shook.

"See we made the earth move." Rick said, sleepily.

Conor sat up quickly. "*Càran,* I think dat was real."

They quickly got off the bed. Calleigh wrapped the sheet around her nakedness. Conor and Rick pulled on their shorts. They moved over toward the sliding door and pushed the curtains aside.

"Oh my God!" Calleigh yelled.

Her eyes were seeing things that her brain didn't understand. A giant fireball erupted into the sky. The ground shook as another explosion sent a shock wave across the island. Their room in Waikiki looked out across the city. A city that now glowed orange not with the sunsets it was so famous for, but giant balls of fire.

Vic grasped Miranda's hand as he looked out across the island and saw several gigantic explosions shoot up into the air.

"Vic!" Miranda screamed along with several others who currently stood on the top platform of the extreme water slide.

A third fireball shot up into the air. This one much closer, somewhere near, or maybe even at the airport.

"What is happening?" Miranda shouted.

"I don't know, Princess. I don't know, but we've got to get down from here."

Vic saw people were crowding the steps, waiting to take the plunge down the massive tunnel and into the tornado funnel. Everyone was looking around trying to identify the source of the thundering sounds.

"Is it an earthquake?" One man asked.

"Maybe a volcano erupted." A woman said.

"No, no. O'ahu doesn't have any active volcanoes. Maybe it was a bomb." Another woman stated.

And that's when all hell broke loose. He looked at Miranda, who stared out across the island, her fingers gripping his almost as tightly as when Charlie had been making his way into the world. Vic counted multiple explosions.

"You know the fastest way out of here, right?" he asked.

Miranda nodded and set their two-person raft at the starting gate of the tunnel. Vic climbed on and gave it a push. His stomach dropped almost faster than the raft, through the hundred and thirty-foot tunnel, out of concern for his friends, who were all currently spread out across the island.

At any other moment he would have been enjoying and trying to prolong the thrill ride that sent them spiraling through the massive funnel, but each turn seemed to take longer than the one before and Vic tried to steer the raft in a more vertical trajectory to get to the bottom faster.

"We have to find Chase and the kids!" Miranda shouted.

Vic nodded. The plan had been to meet up in another twenty minutes at the wave pool, but clearly that would not work. It wouldn't do them any good to go running around the park like mad people along with thousands of others.

They found a staff member ready to receive their raft at the end. "Please head towards Luau Lagoon."

"But we have to find our husband and kids!" Miranda shouted.

"Ma'am, emergency procedures are in effect. Everyone is being directed to the lagoon for safety. Your husband and kids will be there."

Vic nodded and followed the quickly moving crowd toward the grassy area where private parties were usually held. He kept scanning the crowd for familiar faces, but there was no sign of Chase's blond head over the mass of people or the sounds of his kid's voices through the scared crowd.

His bare feet were getting abraded on the concrete as they speed-walked down the pathways lined with employees guiding locals and tourists who had come to the park to enjoy a fun day. When they finally crossed under the archway, instead of feeling safe, Vic only felt an overwhelming sense of frustration. He understood the water park's attempt to control crowds, but the concentration of people in a confined space appeared foolish amidst the island-wide coordinated attack.

He needed to find Chase, get the kids, get their stuff and find a way back to the group. Although he was an excellent doctor, he had no experience surviving attacks like Ryan, Logan, or Clay. They needed to be together.

"Vic, I see them!" Miranda shouted as she pulled him in the opposite direction he'd been looking.

His gaze landed on Chase, who held Charlie in his arms. Standing next to him were Alannah and Gabriella, who held hands. But he didn't see the other boys.

Miranda ran the last several feet and took Gabriella in her arms. "Are you okay, baby?"

"I'm fine, Mom, but what's going on?"

"Well..." Miranda looked over her shoulder at Vic.

"Where's the other three?"

"They were on the Surfsliders while we were in the wave pool. I tried to find them on the way here, but didn't see them."

Vic gave Chase a hard hug and Charlie a kiss. "Everyone stay here. I'll look for them. If we split up, we'll never find each other again." He looked around for a meeting spot. "Better yet, make your way over to the restrooms by the entrance. I'll find the boys and we'll meet you there."

Chase leaned in and whispered. "I think we need to find a way back to the others. I don't know what the fuck is going on, but I think we'll be stronger as a group."

Vic nodded. "I saw four explosions across the island from the top of the Tornado. The closest was near the airport, and the others were scattered around Honolulu. We don't want to take the kids anywhere near danger, but we need to make contact. We're not trained for this, but some of them are."

Miranda stood with the girls clinging to either side of her. "How can we get a phone? All our stuff is locked up in the lockers in the middle of the park."

"I'll figure something out. Now let's move, slowly. Don't make it obvious that we're trying to find a way out of here. I'll meet you there with the boys."

Vic took off in the opposite direction. "Michael, Brandon, Deshawn!" he called out as he wove through the crowd.

He didn't bother to ask anyone if they'd seen the boys because all the faces in the crowd held the same expression. Confusion, fear, and self-preservation.

"Michael and Brandon McGuire! Deshawn Harrison-Ashton!"

After several minutes of constant yelling and working his way through the crowd, his heart rate had climbed for reasons other than physical exertion. Sweat ran down his bare back, and his feet burned from the cuts and scrapes that covered the soles.

"Uncle Vic!"

He whipped his head around toward the sound of three childish voices. There stood his nephews, surrounded by a sea of adults, all ignoring them. And that pissed Vic off because in a situation like this wouldn't a reasonable adult be concerned at finding three young bleeding boys, with scared faces standing alone.

Wait, bleeding?

He ran over and gathered them in his arms. Finally, he felt the first full breath of air fill his lungs since seeing the explosions go off in the distance.

He kneeled on the ground and examined Michael's side. A four-inch laceration marred his flesh above the waistband of his trunks. The cut didn't seem to extend beyond the dermis, so his blood supply wasn't affected, but Vic needed to stop the bleeding. Too bad his swimsuit didn't contain a suture kit and gauze.

He turned and saw a young woman standing near them. "I'm sorry, but can I use the bottom part of your suit?"

"What?" she exclaimed.

Vic pointed to Michael's side. "He's cut badly, and I need to stop the bleeding. I just need a small strip off the bottom of your top."

"Oh, sorry, I thought you meant something else. How do we get it off?"

Vic stood up. "Does anyone have something I can cut with?"

"I've got a small pocket knife," a man said, holding out the implement.

"Perfect." He held it out to the woman. "Would you like to do it? I don't want to get too personal."

She took the knife and cut a fairly even strip off the lower half of her tankini. At least, that's what he thought he'd heard Miranda call that style once. When the woman handed it to him, Vic wrapped it around the boy's stomach. Michael sucked in his breath and gripped Brandon's hand tighter.

"I'm sorry, buddy. But it has to be tight to stop the bleeding. What happened?" he asked.

"We were going down the wicked-cool slide when a bunch of other kids came crashing into us. It was freakin' crazy cause we were all stuck together and getting tossed up the sides around the curves. When we landed, Michael looked like a stuck pig, and Deshawn was gripping his knee like a wide receiver taken out by a three hundred pound defenseman."

Vic noticed Michael had his arm around Deshawn, and the boy was favoring his right leg. Vic did a quick assessment of the injury. There didn't appear to be anything broken.

"Can you walk, Deshawn?"

"Yes, sir."

"We'll help him, Uncle Vic," Michael said.

"Okay, here's the plan. We're going to make our way to the edge of the crowd and meet everyone else by the bathroom near the entrance."

"What's going on, Uncle Vic? Why did they stick us all in here like a herd of cattle?" Brandon asked.

Vic saw several adult heads turn their way at the question. Now that immediate safety was not an issue, the people were getting restless with no information or plan coming from the water park staff.

He gathered the boys in close and lowered his voice. "I'm going to tell you because I need your help keeping the little ones calm, okay?"

Three heads nodded, and the man next to them, who'd volunteered his pocket knife, shuffled closer.

"There were some explosions on the island. I don't know at this point whether there was a bad accident or if someone did it on purpose. We need to get ahold of your parents. Deshawn, I'm hoping your dad can get us some information and tell us what we should do."

"Hey man, shouldn't we stay here? Safety in numbers and all?" The man next to him asked.

Vic nodded. He didn't want any tagalongs. "You should. My friend is with the FBI, and that's the only reason I'm going to try to contact him. I'm just getting a cell phone, then coming back. He'll be able to tell us the best course of action."

The man nodded. "Good. Then you'll tell these people because I don't think they have a clue."

Vic guided the boys to the edge of the crowd. It became apparent that Deshawn's knee was giving him more problems than he wanted to let on. He needed to get the boy to a hospital for an MRI, and Michael needed stitches. There was a first aid station near the lockers, but he doubted it was supplied for this type of situation.

"I see them," Brandon yelled. He tried to run ahead, but Michael had hold of his hand. Brandon looked over his shoulder at his twin and immediately put his arm around him.

Michael was looking pale under his recently acquired tan, and the makeshift bandage that Vic had made of the woman's swimsuit was red.

This is bad.

He waved to Chase and Miranda. When he was close enough that he didn't have to yell and get the attention of others loitering in the area, he said, "Change of plans. We need to get these two to a hospital."

"How are we going to do that? I doubt the staff is going to let us just walk out of here." Chase said. He pointed to the archway entrance. "They're standing guard like a couple of Roman centurions."

"And judging by what we saw, EMS is tied up with bigger problems." Miranda added.

"All right, then we're about to go stealth." He turned towards the kids. "Are you prepared to accept this mission, my little soldiers?"

Five heads nodded, and the two girls plus Charlie giggled.

"Right, I want the rest of you to go around the back side of the bathroom and sneak past the entrance while I distract our guards with the explanation that I need to get access to the first aid station."

"Which is conveniently right next to the lockers." Chase added.

"M'hm. While I'm getting our stuff, make your way to the front entrance."

He kneeled down so he was at eye level with his kids. "Your jobs are to be on the lookout for anyone in red shirts and tell mommy and papa." He looked at Michael and Brandon. "Can I count on you to get your sister to the exit?"

"Yes, sir." Brandon said with a little salute.

"Excellent. Our operation is a go."

"Wait, can we have like a secret code word or signal or something?" Brandon asked.

"That's a terrific idea." Chase said.

Vic looked at Michael and Deshawn. "Any ideas?"

Deshawn smiled. "My papa always says he needs to 'bang out a contract' when he wants to talk to dad about something and they don't want me to hear."

Vic tried to keep a straight face while Miranda and Chase high fived behind the kids' backs.

"Good one," Chase said softly.

"Great suggestion, Deshawn. I'll be sure to tell your papa it was your idea."

After that, they went in their separate directions. Vic noticed that the employees guarding the entrance to the lagoon were furiously tapping on their phones. So that meant there was still a signal available. That was good news for him.

"Excuse me, I'm Doctor Burns, and my nephew has been injured. I need to get access to your first-aid station."

"Um, we're not supposed to let anyone out of here. Maybe I can go get what you need and bring it back?"

Vic felt for the teenager, but he had a mission. "Really? Do you know the difference between Steri-strip elastic skin closures and Tegaderm mesh dressing?"

The former of which doesn't apply in Michael's case, but they don't need to know that.

"We have SpongeBob Band-Aids and Solarcaine?"

He saw the rest of the group sneaking past them, and Brandon gave Vic a thumbs up. Vic sighed. "Please, just let me go find what I need to help my nephew. I promise not to say anything and get you in trouble. I mean, if you really want, just turn your backs and I'll sneak out."

The two employees looked at each other, then looked down at their phones. Vic took that as his signal and stepped around them. He quickly made his way past the various attractions, keeping an eye out for any employees who were patrolling the grounds. He felt very Mission Impossible. A stop at the first aid station revealed that the teenage guards weren't joking regarding the minimal supplies. He saw nothing there that would help Michael more than his improvised bandage.

He did a quick area check after he stepped out of the station, then made for the locker area. Their group had commandeered two family-sized lockers so they could run around and not worry about important items going missing. He grabbed his cell phone and turned it on.

Vic tried calling Matt first, but got no response. Then he tried Niall and Trevor. Again, straight to voicemail. There wasn't time to mess around. He needed to get to the entrance and find the others. Arms full of clothes, wallets, cell phones, car keys and a purse, he gave up on stealth and made a dash for the entrance.

"Vic!" Chase called out.

He saw his partner standing on the far side of the gate behind a potted palm tree and veered left. When he arrived, Chase caught him, and Vic almost dropped all his booty with the desire to wrap his arms around the man he loved.

"I've got you," Chase whispered.

Their mouths met, and Chase's arms secured him until Vic stopped shaking. Chase's kisses had been making his knees weak for the last two decades, but right now the tremble in his legs was because this situation was scarier than he was willing to admit in front of Miranda and the kids.

Chase pulled away from their kiss and leaned his forehead against Vic's. "I've needed that from the moment I saw you on the field. I told Miranda to get the kids to the van. Let's get the fuck out of here."

Vic handed Chase his phone and wallet. "I tried Matt, Niall, and Trevor but got no response. You keep trying to get ahold of them. I'm going to call Logan and Clay."

Chase nodded as they started across the parking lot. He clicked the unlock and remote start button on the keyfob. As soon as the doors opened on the van the group rented, they piled inside. Miranda masterfully coordinated seatbelts and booster seats and sat in the backseat to keep the kids as calm as possible. He and Chase climbed in, and Vic got behind the wheel.

"Where should we go?" Miranda asked.

"The hospitals are probably only taking major trauma cases. Chase, can you look up the nearest urgent care or clinic?"

"Already on it. It looks like the closest one that is open right now is the Kunia Urgent Care. Go East on H1 to H750 North then turn right on Kupuohi St in Village Park. About ten minutes." He turned to look at Michael and Deshawn. "Hang on guys, we're going to get you fixed up."

Vic nodded. As they took off, he connected the phone to Bluetooth and told the hands - free system to dial Clay.

"Hello?"

"Clay? Thank God. Listen fast, we have a situation. I saw at least four explosions across the island. Three across the bay and one somewhere near the airport. Where are you and Logan?"

"I know. We saw Waikiki go up as we were heading back to port, but from out here we can't tell exactly where or what happened. I've been trying to get ahold of everybody, but none of you assholes were picking up your phones!"

"We were still at the water park, and they corralled us into one area. We locked up our stuff. But we escaped and are now in the van. We're headed for an urgent care since Michael and Deshawn are injured. Nothing life-threatening, but we need to get it taken care of."

"Copy that. We're still on the boat. But the captain has been acting weird, circling the bay and talking on the radio a lot."

"Probably trying to find out if he should dock or keep you guys out there. You took off from Aloha Tower Marketplace, and that's right between Waikiki and the airport. I haven't been able to reach Matt, Niall, or Trevor."

"Weren't they going on some kind of hike or something? I bet they don't have cell reception."

"Maybe, but I still don't want them coming down into some kind of war zone, which is exactly what it looked like from what I saw."

"I'll keep trying to reach the guys. What about Conor's clan?"

"We've got all the kids. Calleigh, Rick, and Conor were having a private afternoon at the hotel. Chase is trying to reach them now."

"Which is right in the fucking center of Waikiki."

Vic sighed. "Yeah. But we just have to keep trying." He glanced back at Michael, Brandon, and Alannah. He lowered his voice. "The older kids know something happened, but we're trying to keep the little ones on a need to know basis. I gave them only enough info to stop the constant questions."

"We'll find everyone. We have to." Clay said.

"I think our best option after getting Michael and Deshawn taken care of is to get in touch with Ryan. Maybe he has some contacts on the island that can tell him what the hell is going on."

"Good idea. Since you have his son, he'll probably want to hear from you."

"That's my next call. I'll text you—"

The phone went dead, and Vic saw that there was no longer a signal. He looked back at Chase, who shook his head.

"Well, shit."

Chapter Eight

♥

R yan paced Steven's office. The local agents were all on phones, working contacts trying to figure out what the hell was happening. Reports of the explosions had come in almost an hour ago. Ryan had still been at the office working with Noelani on scenarios when all their theories had become reality.

"Were you able to get in touch with Ethan?" Steven asked.

"No, and I can't reach our friends at the water park, either. It's only a couple of miles from here, and I'm doing everything I can not to just run out the door and go after them."

"I know. I'm fighting the same urge not to go after my family, but we have a job to do and are more equipped to understand what's going on than the local HPD. All the bombs have detonated far away from our location, so I'm sure your son is fine."

It royally sucked, but Steven was right. The faster they caught the fuckers doing this, the faster he could get back to his family. It didn't change his need to hear Ethan and Deshawn's voices.

"Bring me up to speed on the situation."

"We have six confirmed detonations. A plane waiting to depart for San Francisco exploded on the tarmac, a truck bomb detonated in front of the Prince Kūhiō Federal Building, Hawaii Convention

Center has been nearly obliterated, and three of the nine wastewater plants on the island. If there is any small bit of good news, initial assessments show that none of the detonations contained radioactive material."

"Jesus Christ. Transportation, government, tourism, and water supply. The only thing they forgot was—"

The building shook with a great thundering roar, and Ryan got thrown to the ground. He screamed as Steven's bookcase came down on top of him, tried to cover his face as fluorescent lights exploded over his head and glass from the windows blew every which way. Drywall dust filled his lungs, but the only things he saw were Ethan and Deshawn's faces.

I love you.

The building continued to vibrate, and people screamed. He couldn't tell where the epicenter of the explosion was, but at least he wasn't falling into a crater to be buried under thousands of tons of material. Several minutes passed, and Ryan realized his time on this planet wasn't ending.

Thank you.

"Ryan!"

He coughed and tried to push the bookshelf off but didn't have the right leverage.

"Ryan!"

"I'm here ... I'm here. You okay?"

"Damn golf trophy hit me on the head, but I'll survive. I can't see shit. Where are you?"

"Underneath the damn bookcase your trophy was sitting on. I'm pinned."

He heard some shuffling around, then the weight on his chest eased and he rolled out from beneath his prison. Ryan took stock of all his extremities. Nothing was missing so that was good. He felt battered and bruised but with no serious injuries. He looked over at Steven, who had blood dripping down the side of his face.

"Shit, that looks bad."

Steven put a hand on top of his head and groaned. "Head wounds always look worse than they are. Probably a mild concussion, if anything. I'm fine. Let's go assess the damage."

They pushed furniture out of the way to get to the door. Ryan pulled the door open and came face to face with Noelani.

"Sir, we have several wounded from debris but no severe casualties on this floor."

Steven stepped out of his office. "Good." Suddenly, a loud alarm went off. "Well fuck. This just got better."

"What is that for?"

"It's the automatic chemical agent alarm."

"Are you fucking kidding me?"

"Nope. Noelani, gather who you can find on this floor and get them out of the building. I'll go down to the floors below with Ryan and do the same."

"Yes, Sir."

Noelani moved, calling out for everyone still on the floor to follow her. He watched as a handful of agents and personnel gathered in front of the emergency exit. Dirty and disheveled, but all in one piece, they made their way out the door.

Ryan looked at Steven. "What are you thinking? The emergency response protocol ensures there is an agent on every floor in charge of evacuation. We should help Noelani get these people out."

"Look around. There's not a lot of structural damage, but the place is a wreck, and now with the alarm protocol requires us to evacuate until all systems can be cleared. Something just doesn't seem right to me."

"This whole day doesn't seem right, but what's got your nose twitching about this particular event?"

"I'm not sure yet, but it feels as though whoever did this didn't want to kill us per se, but just keep us distracted. I want to know why?"

"And the potential chemical agent that is even now filling our lungs with poison?"

"A red herring."

"Okay, Scooby Doo, I'll bite. What next?"

"We clear the building as procedure calls for, but we just make a few stops along the way."

Ryan saw the locker that held the bureau's tactile gear. He stopped by and grabbed two gas masks, communication units, vests, a Glock 22, and some extra magazines. He made the weapon ready and turned to face Steven.

"Better safe than sorry."

Steven did the same with his weapon and accepted the extra gear. They aimed for the staircase on the opposite side from where Mahi'ai led the group. When they reached the stairwell, the power went out. Their only way to navigate came from the strobe lights attached to the silent fire alarms. He followed Steven's shadow, which was blurry through the plastic of his mask. They cleared the floor beneath them, but didn't encounter anyone. Which was eerie given how crowded and busy it had been earlier. They'd encountered a lot of broken windows and downed ceiling panels. Ryan studied a couple of the internal support columns with a careful eye as they were missing large chunks, but seemed to hold. They went down another set of stairs, putting them on the second level, and Ryan felt a change in the atmosphere.

Steven entered the office area on the second floor, and Ryan blinked several times. Despite the gas mask, his nose filled with the scent of burning construction material and fire retardant. The automatic systems had done their job so that they weren't trapped in an inferno, but Ryan hissed as his suit offered no protection from the high temperature of small fires still burning.

"Look out!" Steven yelled.

Ryan froze and looked down. He'd nearly stepped into a gaping hole. He could see down to the lobby.

"Fuck me. Thanks. This must be where the bomb went off."

He looked around for casualties, but miraculously there were none either whole or in pieces. Nothing like what Ryan had come across when investigating previous bombings. Some of which still haunted his nightmares.

They made it to the lobby, and Ryan thought Steven was about to vacate the premises, but instead he crossed the shelled-out building. Ryan would be lying if he weren't a tad nervous walking right through the middle of the building. He looked up at the jagged edges of what used to be a decorative ceiling. At least the stairwells had provided some structural support should things go from bad to worse. After scaling over some debris, they made it to the far side of the building. Steven brought out a metal key and entered a sixteen-digit code on a manual lock panel. Ryan had one just like it at his office.

"The server room?"

"Just the access. We have to go down another set of stairs and through the secured doors. There should be nobody down here. All the agents whose work is in direct connection with it or our other IT systems have offices on the third floor, which we already cleared."

They descended step by step into pitch darkness. The air felt very artificial after clearing all the levels above with blown-out windows.

Steven entered another set of codes at the secured doors, and they stepped into a pristine room. Ryan had to blink several times to adjust to the bright light. Ryan thought he saw movement, so he signaled to Steven. They began a sweep of the area with Steven taking the left and Ryan taking the right. The server bays were long rows of mesh-front lockers. The server lights glowed, and the temperature dropped here.

"Why is there still power and HAVC running in here when the rest of the building is out?"

"Self-contained system. Generators that maintain a constant supply supplement the power 24/7 and this entire room has precision air conditioning that controls temperature, humidity, and air particle filtration within some crazy tolerance levels I don't understand."

Ryan stopped when he turned a corner and noticed the door to one of the server bays was open. There wasn't anybody standing there, but given it was the only one open so far, that didn't seem right. The other thing he noticed was that there was no damage from the bombs where they were. So again, it appeared there had been an almost surgical approach to the locations. Was it possible Kyung had an inside man?

Weapon ready, he made his way down the aisle. He was about half-way to the open bay when someone slammed him into the lockers on the other side. Ryan's ears rang and his vision blurred when his facemask met the assailant's foot. He'd dropped his weapon, but didn't bother searching for it. He tried a series of elbow and knee strikes, but received vicious kicks to his ribs and kidneys for his efforts. The man was well-trained.

Ryan noticed his attacker wasn't wearing any body armor and his mask was more of the concealment variety versus protection. He concentrated his efforts on hitting the target areas of the body and aimed for the pressure points. It was a good test of muscle memory from all those years of training both in the Navy and as a field agent.

What do you know it's kind of like riding a bicycle? And where the fuck is Steven?

He got the advantage and had their guy on the ground. Ryan was fed up with this whole day and directed his frustrations toward the only person who was responsible so far.

"FBI, don't move!"

He looked up, saw that Steven had finally arrived and had his weapon trained on their suspect's head. Ryan ripped off the man's mask.

"Patterson! You son-of-a-bitch." Steven said as he ripped off his mask.

Patterson laughed, thrust up and tried to dislodge Ryan. Good thing he hadn't let go of his grip.

"Get off him, Ryan. He's not going anywhere now."

Ryan looked up at Steven. His friend seemed in control despite the vicious scowl on his face. He wasn't taking any chances, though. He flipped Patterson over, but then realized he had nothing to secure him with.

"Give me your shoelaces." He told Steven.

Ryan saw his weapon near his left knee and retrieved it and held it against Patterson's back least he think of trying something while Steven got them some improvised handcuffs.

He looped the laces around Patterson's wrists and tied a knot that would at least get them to the exits.

"Do you idiots actually think you've saved the fucking day?" Patterson asked.

"We got you, didn't we?" Steven responded.

Patterson laughed again. "You're too late, and I'm expendable."

"What did you do?"

"That's for me to know and for you to figure out. I'm not going to lay here and give you a monologue with all the answers wrapped up in a fucking pretty bow for you to present to the dictators who run this fucked up country. Now I'm going to shut up, and you are going to walk me out of here."

Ryan did not like the way Patterson sounded. Too calm. Too in control. Too self-assured. But unfortunately, there was nothing more they could do at this point. Steven was going to have to get his tech on the job from a remote location to figure out exactly what Patterson was doing in the server room. Chances were, it was nothing good. They stood him up and made their way back toward the stairwell. Ryan had lost his mask in the fight, but since none of them were dead, it appeared the alarm really had been false to get all the agents out of the building.

"Let's take him out the back. I don't want to draw attention with all the personnel who gathered outside."

"Good idea. Until we know more, let's keep all the information contained as much as we can. Who knows, there might be another mole waiting for us out there."

Ryan blinked as the midday sun hit him the moment they exited the building. Patterson's body jerked, spraying Ryan's face and neck with warm fluid, before he could ask Steven which way to go. Instinct kicked in, and he dropped to the ground.

"Shots fired ... shots fired!"

Patterson lay on the ground with half of his head blown off. Ryan left him where he was and commando crawled over to a low wall that surrounded the building. He looked around for Steven and found him pinned to the wall on the opposite side of the courtyard. Ryan reached up and wiped away the blood and brain matter that had landed on him.

"Ryan, you good?" Steven shouted.

"Fan-fucking-tastic. You?"

"Could use a latte. Maybe a muffin."

Ryan scoffed and flicked Steven off. There had been no further shots since the one that had taken out Patterson, but he wasn't in the mood to play gopher. He took out his cell and noticed that there wasn't a signal.

Great.

They couldn't stay down here forever. He looked back at what was left of Patterson. It would take an evidence response team to analyze the caliber and trajectory of the shot, but Ryan placed his bet on a long distance and a very hot charge. The problem was where the shot had come from? The building's design made it so there was green space on both sides and no taller buildings in the immediate vicinity. Not a sniper's playground. He looked up at the sky.

He knew the bureau, military, and other law enforcement agencies had validated Helicopter Aerial Rifle Marksmanship (HARM) classes—the tactic had even been utilized a few times in the last couple of years. Ryan didn't remember hearing the telltale sound of rotors in the air, but for a well-trained sniper the shot could have come from as far as eighteen hundred yards away.

He heard a sound coming from his left and spun with his weapon raised.

"Hold your fire, FBI!"

Ryan saw a man holding up his badge. "Yeah? So was he," he said, pointing to Patterson. "And he caused all this shit."

So much for keeping the information contained, Ashton.

"It's okay, Ryan. That's agent Barnes."

"Sir, we've cleared the immediate area."

"That shot must have come from the air. I want you to contact Hickam Field and have the Air Force scan for any birds in the air. With the airport closed, there should be nothing in the sky right now. If there is find out where the fuck they're going."

"Yes, Sir!"

Ryan stood, and he and Steven made their way back toward Patterson's body. "Guess he really was disposable."

Steven rubbed the back of his neck. "This is ... fuck, I don't even know. All I see is my balls in a vice from the director, not to mention we still have to figure out what the fuck is going on and why."

"Well, you need to set up a temporary command first. Clearly, the building is non-operational. We need to find Noelani. And you need to get in contact with your teams onsite at the other bomb locations. And I need to find my husband and son."

"Will it do me any good to remind you that you're on vacation?"

Ryan just stared at Steven, who shrugged his shoulders.

"I had to ask."

Ethan kept looking down at his phone willing the signal icon to light up, but the systems were so screwed that he had little hope. He had to find a way to contact Ryan and Deshawn. He had to make sure they were safe. God knew his husband usually had the unique talent of finding himself involved in terrorist plots on a far too frequent basis.

But now it was *him* that found himself smack dab in the middle of a nightmare.

He was having a hard time focusing since his ears were still ringing, and he was dizzy.

Jesus is this what it's like for Logan? No, *Logan can't hear at all, I can hear it's just mishmash. Okay concentrate.*

He looked around the area and started to tear up. The grounds surrounding the Aliolani Hale were littered with people. Some bleeding, some crying, all covered in dirt and dust from the explosion that had decimated the Federal Building a block over.

He'd been doing some sightseeing in the capitol district, taking pictures of the historic buildings they used in Hawaii 5-0, when he'd flown through the air and been thrown to the ground. It felt as though the ground beneath his feet should have opened up and swallowed him whole. Then seconds later, great plumes of smoke filled the air. That's when he'd heard the first screams. It had taken him several minutes to figure out exactly what had happened.

Shards and bits of glass from buildings in the area covered the ground after exploding outward, and raining over anyone in their path. Now he sat. Waiting. Waiting to be told what to do. Waiting to find the courage to ask questions about how many were injured or killed. Waiting to accept how a place of such beauty now resembled the gates of hell. He saw another fire truck race down the street, and standing next to him was a young man, staring towards the shell of what was part of the Prince Kūhiō Federal Building.

"Are you okay?"

The man looked over to where clouds of dust rose in the air. "That was my office. I ... I was on my way back after a meeting."

He swallowed. "You ... you, um. I don't know. What do you do?"

"Attorney. US District Court of Hawaii. Assistant to Judge Wilson."

Ethan laughed, and the guy speared him with a look of pure rage. Understandable, since the guy's boss had probably just died.

He held up his hands. "No, no, not what you think." He held out his hand. "Ethan Harrison. Assistant US Attorney D. Mass. Apparently, I can't even get away from the job while on vacation."

They shook hands and continued to stare at the sky, where smoke filled the air. He could see only part of the building since the complex extended down the block, but it didn't take a Harvard graduate to figure out that he'd been extremely lucky.

"Hey, is your phone working? I'm sorry I don't know your name."

"It's Kale Palakiko. And no it's not. I forgot to plug it in last night and my battery ran down during my meeting."

"Well Kale, I hope your boss and co-workers are okay, but I have to go."

"Where! The fucking island is under attack. I heard that there were at least six bombs that went off around the city."

Ethan noticed that the people sitting around them all looked their direction, and many whose faces had been masks of defeat morphed into terror.

"Hey! Calm down. Yelling and getting everyone frightened is not going to make this situation better. I don't know where I'm going to go, but I can't stay here. I need to find my family and friends. I've got a scooter parked on the other side of the palace. I'm going to ride until I get a signal, then I'll figure out the next step."

"Can I come with you?"

Jesus, he didn't know what to say. Clearly the kid was terrified, but the last thing Ethan needed right now was someone following him around like a lost puppy. But he didn't feel right just walking away either.

"You can join me until we find a signal. Then, you can contact your family. You have one here on the island, right?"

Kale nodded. "My parents live in Pearl City."

"Good. Then we'll somehow find you a way back to them."

Ethan started walking towards the Iolani Palace. He hoped his scooter was still where he'd left it, but if not, then he'd figure out something else.

They reached the parking lot, and Ethan let out a sigh of relief. He pointed to the neon green and black moped. "That's it. Technically, only one rider is allowed at a time, but I think the cops have other problems on their hands. If you promise not to prosecute us, then so will I."

He heard the kid chuckle and smiled. Good. A little levity was needed to keep the tears at bay. Ethan wasn't even ready to think about the scale of the tragedy that had just hit the island.

He climbed on and slid forward so that Kale could perch on the back half of the seat. "Since I'm the Haole, what direction do you think is the best?"

"Do you know where your family is?"

"My husband is with the FBI and was called in to consult on some tip. I guess we now know what. My son is with some friends at the Wet 'n' Wild water park."

"Both are across the bay northwest of here. I guess the logical thing would be to head in that direction. However, I don't really think this little thing is designed for highways."

As much as his heart raced to reach Ryan and Deshawn as quickly as possible, he knew Kale was right.

"We have another car back at our hotel. But that's down in Waikiki. And I can't even guarantee it's there since I had some other friends who had use of it today, and they may have taken it out. What were you saying about other bombs?"

Kale's eyes darted around. "I … it's just what I heard."

"Well, did you hear where?"

"Um … I think they said the convention center?"

"If you're right, then how would we even get to Waikiki? The route I took to get here went right past that place."

"We would just have to go the long way around. I can give you directions, but I think we need that car. I'm sorry."

Ethan nodded. He started up the scooter and said a silent prayer for his family.

I'm coming guys. I promise.

Trevor opened the car door so fast that it bounced back at him as Matt came to a stop near the emergency room.

"Help! Somebody I need help!"

There were people everywhere, but nobody responded to his yell.

"Hey! I need a doctor."

Matt came around the front of the car and surveyed the area. "Something's not right. This looks more like a triage station than ER entrance. Let's get him inside ourselves."

It had taken them much longer than Trevor was comfortable with to get Niall down the mountain. Now it was almost dusk, and his lover had been slowly deteriorating for the past several hours. Niall had gone from making occasional groans to silence, and his complexion was more of a gray than the dusky tan that Trevor was used to seeing. Matt had forced them to stop on the trail every so often to check Niall's pulse, respirations, and the bandage. But now they were here, and it looked like half of Honolulu was as well.

What the fuck is going on?

They brought out the makeshift litter and got Niall settled, then carried him towards the door. A security officer saw them and signaled for them to stop.

"I'm Dr. Lincoln, and I have a 40 - year-old male with a GSW to the chest by rifle approximately six hours ago. He has a pneumothorax to the right lung, his pulse is thirty-five, and he's most likely in hypovolemic shock."

The guard flagged them through and spoke into his radio as Trevor went past. As soon as they got past the doors, a team of nurses and doctors rushed to meet them. Before he could say a word, they whisked Niall away.

I love you. Come back to us.

He looked around the emergency room of the Queens Medical Center in shock. Dozens of people took up every spare inch of space. Moans, whimpers, and cries came at him with various intensity

He walked up to a harried-looking nurse. "What's going on?"

She stared at him. "Sir, we're doing the best we can. Please have a seat, and someone will be with you soon."

Then she ran off as a code blue announcement came over the speaker. Where was Matt? He looked around but didn't see his other partner. Trevor wrapped his arms around his waist, unsure of what to do. Where to go.

"*Bello.*"

He spun around and latched onto Matt. Whose arms came around him and Trevor lost the ability to hold anything in for a second longer. His body shook, and he couldn't stop the tears from soaking Matt's shirt.

"Tell me we'll see him again. Alive! Tell me we'll see him alive."

Matt guided him to the only empty corner in the area. "He's so strong. He made it down a mountain with a hole through his chest and a collapsed lung for the past six hours. If anyone can survive that, it's Niall."

He glanced around at the over-occupied waiting area. "What happened, Matt?"

"Terrorists. Apparently, there was some kind of coordinated attack. Several bombs went off within minutes of each other. The hospital has been taking casualties all day."

"Oh, my God! We have to find everyone." Trevor took out his phone, but the battery was almost gone. "Do you have power?"

Matt nodded. "I've already tried Ryan and Ethan, but there was no answer. Let's try Logan and Clay."

Trevor bit his nails while waiting for Matt's call to be answered. He checked his phone again. Maybe enough juice for one call. But who should it be? Rick? Chase? Calleigh?

"Logan, it's good to hear your voice."

Trevor whipped his head around at the sound of Matt's voice. "Is he safe? Is he with Clay? Where are they?"

Matt took Trevor's hand and gave it a squeeze. "I'm with Trevor at Queen's Medical Center ... no, we're okay, but someone shot Niall."

Oh God, Niall.

Trevor looked toward the curtained area where the medical team had taken him. He strained to hear any sounds that might give a clue what was happening, but there was nothing more than the organized confusion of a crowded emergency room.

"We don't know yet. They took him up to surgery right away..."

They did? When?

"That's good. We're headed up to the surgical floor waiting area. We'll see you soon." Matt hung up the phone. "They're fine. They were out on the boat when it all happened. The port authority only let them dock a little while ago. They're coming here, and we're going to work on finding everyone else. Now we need to get you some water, and you need to sit down. I can tell you're dehydrated and about to fall off your feet."

Words refused to leave his mouth. At least he knew that two of his friends were alive. Matt led him by the hand to a bank of elevators. Trevor felt more of his energy draining with each second. He leaned against Matt's side once his partner had selected the floor he assumed they were supposed to go to. Matt put his arm around him and kissed the top of his head.

The ding of the elevator sounded like a gong. With each step, his feet shuffled more, and by the time he saw a bank of chairs, Trevor knew it was going to be close.

"You're okay, *Bello*. It's just the adrenaline leaving you. Close your eyes if you need to. I'm here."

His eyes fluttered closed, but he jerked his head up. He needed to be awake when they got news of Niall. He needed to see Logan and Clay. He looked down and saw the phone app was still open on his phone.

Who was I going to call earlier?

Upstairs was markedly quieter than downstairs. He looked over at the nurses' station and saw a bunch of numbers on a large monitor. Was one of those random numbers the man he loved? Were the doctors now desperately racing against time to save him, or had the delay been fatal?

Matt held out a bottle of water to Trevor. "Take it. You need fluids." He kneeled in front of Trevor and unscrewed the cap, then held it out to him. "We're going to make it. All of us."

He nodded, weakly.

Chapter Nine

♥

L ogan stepped off the elevator, spying Matt and Trevor right away. He pointed toward them and guided Clay in their direction. Logan met Trevor's gaze, and the man practically jumped three feet in the air.

"Logan!"

He caught Trevor and held him tight.

Thank God he's all in one piece.

He'd never felt as powerless as when he'd seen the bombs go off from the boat. Darkness swirled around him as he watched the island burst into flames. Helpless and terrified, trapped on the water while the city burned. The fate of his found family unknown. He'd pulled out every trick he'd learned in therapy to prevent the threat of flashbacks from taking over.

Clay patted Trevor on the back. "Hey Thumbelina. Good to see you."

Logan let go of Trevor when he pushed on his chest and stepped back.

"I'd bitch you out for calling me that, but I'm just too damn happy to see you, asshole."

Logan and Matt both chuckled. Leave it to Trevor to give someone both a compliment and a dressing-down simultaneously.

"Any news?"

Both Trevor and Matt shook their heads.

"I spoke to Vic not long after it happened. He, Chase, Miranda, and all the kids are together. They're all safe, but had to take Michael and Deshawn for some patching up at an urgent care center." Clay said.

Trevor gasped.

Logan stopped him before Trevor hit him with a barrage of questions. "Nothing critical. Nowhere near the bombs. Things got a little crazy at the water park during, I guess some kind of evacuation. It was hard to catch everything he said because the connection was spotty."

Matt frowned. "I tried them a little while ago, but didn't get an answer. Might have been my phone though. We were still barely in range after coming off the mountain."

They all headed back over to the chairs and sat down. "What the hell happened up there?"

Matt sighed. "I'm still trying to figure it out. We were working our way across the ridgeline towards Manoa Middle when Niall shouted. Someone shot our guide, and he fell off the side of the mountain. We need to notify someone so they can search for his body."

Trevor shivered. "You don't think he's still alive up there, do you?"

"No, *Bello*. He took a shot to the head, remember? We saw it."

Logan rubbed his hands together to ground himself in the here and now. The chance of watching friends be taken out by snipers was a risk he'd had to live with while in the service, but it shouldn't be happening while on vacation. Not here. Not again.

Clay gripped one hand and Trevor the other.

"Take a deep breath, Logan."

He did and let it out. "I'm good. Sorry."

"Nothing to be sorry for. This kind of violence will probably always be one of your triggers. All you can do is maintain your focus and remember to breathe." Matt said.

How did he get so fucking lucky to find friends like this? Here Trevor and Matt sat, waiting to hear if the man they loved was going to live, and they took the time to make *him* feel better. He nodded he was okay. Well, not okay, but he needed to hear the rest of the story. Needed to understand what had happened and try to figure out why.

"It was only a few seconds later that Niall took a bullet to his upper chest. They continued to shoot at Trevor and me for several minutes. I got grazed in the upper arm, and then it went silent."

Clay stood up quickly and pulled at Matt's sleeve. "You're shot too?"

Matt hissed when the fabric of his shirt pulled on his skin. "Graze. There's nothing to be done but get a shot of antibiotics and let it heal. May have even been a shard of rock that got me, not the actual bullet? I never even got a clear idea of where the shots were coming from, or where the person went who made them. It's not like there's a lot of options up there, you know?"

Trevor walked off to the nurses' station, probably trying to round up a doctor for Matt.

Clay looked at Trevor's back then turned to Matt. "I've seen a lot of shit in my time as a homicide cop, and we both know what Logan's been through, but Trevor ... well he's a tough little shit, but not hardened like we are. So I'm asking you to tell it to us straight. Do you think he's going to make it?"

Matt closed his eyes. "I have to believe it." He opened his eyes and stared at Clay. "If he doesn't, then ... God, I don't even know how to finish that sentence."

Logan put his arm around Matt. It was time that he lent his friend some of *his* strength. Matt had been a pillar that Logan had leaned on in his early days of recovery, and now his friend needed him.

Trevor came back with a nurse in tow. "You're going to go with her, and she's going to look at your arm. I don't want to hear any backtalk. And you will do exactly what she says. Got it?"

Matt stood and smiled. "Thank you, *Bello*."

Logan snickered, and Clay rolled his eyes.

Trevor sat down next to Logan.

"You sure told him."

Trevor made a sign that had Clay snickering and Logan questioning his genetic make-up and birthright.

"I think we should try calling the others again. Unfortunately, my phone is dead. You think the hospital will let us use theirs?"

Logan looked down at his phone. It had an app that allowed incoming and outgoing calls to read out across the screen like closed captions. The streaming ability of his cochlear implant processors was great, but sometimes he still misunderstood words.

"I'll try Ryan."

He opened the app and selected the icon to place a call, then tapped on Ryan's name. The screen on his phone indicated that it was dialing his number. He heard the ringtone trill through his processors.

"Ryan? It's Logan."

"Thank God, where are you guys? Have you heard from Ethan or Deshawn?"

"We're with Matt and Trevor at Queen's Medical. I know Deshawn is with Chase's crew and he's safe. They were making a stop at a clinic earlier, but it wasn't anything serious. I think Deshawn banged up his knee during the evacuation. But none of us have been able to reach Ethan, Rick, Conor, or Calleigh."

"Fuck! I haven't been able to either. Do you know where my son is now?"

"Last I heard, they were going to get back to the hotel. Get the kids settled and calm. Have you tried calling Vic or the others?"

"Yes, several times right after it happened. Then, well, let's just say it got a little bumpy around here."

That doesn't sound good.

"I'm glad to hear that Deshawn is safe, but I still really need to hear his voice. I'll try calling the hotel and have them patch me through to the room. But I'm worried sick about Ethan. None of you have spoken to him since it happened?"

"No. I'm sorry, Ry. Have you ... fuck ... have you tried calling the hospitals?"

"Yes, but he's not registered anywhere."

"Where are you?"

"I'm with the special agent in charge of the Honolulu division. We've been working the situation since this morning."

"This morning? You mean before..."

"I can't really talk about it."

"Of course, I'm sorry."

"You said you're at Queen's? Is everyone okay?"

Logan looked over at Trevor. "Not so much. Niall was shot, and he's in surgery right now."

"Shot? When? Where?"

"While on their hike. Matt said they were making their way to the peak when a sniper killed their guide and then shot Niall."

"Hold on for a minute."

Logan heard Ryan talking to someone in the background but couldn't make out the words. He felt Trevor tense up next to him and saw a doctor walking in their general direction.

"Look, Logan. I need to talk to Matt and Trevor. It's possible that what happened to them is connected to the attacks today. I know this is not a good time, but do you think they're up to answering questions?"

He saw Matt walking toward them from the opposite direction of the doctor, and Trevor gripped his leg, tightly.

"I think we're about to get word on Niall."

"Put me on speaker."

Logan put his hand on Trevor's shoulder. "Ryan wants to hear. Can I put him on speaker?"

Trevor nodded, then got up and ran over to Matt. Logan tapped the button to switch modes, then joined them. Clay's presence behind him settled his nerves somewhat.

"Dr. Lincoln? I'm Dr. McKeever. You're the one who brought in Mr. Roberge? It surprised me to hear that you'd stayed."

"Perhaps they didn't give you all the information because of the emergency. Mr. Roberge is my partner." He held up Trevor and his linked hands. "Our partner."

"Oh, I see. That certainly makes more sense. I was just told that a doctor brought in an unconscious man suffering from a gunshot wound. As you can imagine, we've had many people arriving in groups today. Well, I'm happy to report that he made it through the surgery."

Trevor and Matt both let out a long breath.

"Given the type of injury and length of time between the incident and his admission, that's pretty remarkable. I'll be honest, it came close a time or two during the procedure. At one point his blood pressure dropped rapidly, and we had no choice but to open his chest. We discovered that when the bullet passed through his body, it nicked a rib, and during the surgery one of the fragments must have shifted, slicing into the internal thoracic artery. He hemorrhaged, but we were able to close it off, and he stabilized. When you go see him, I want you to be prepared to see a tube running out of his chest. That is allowing any remaining blood and air in his chest to drain so his lung can re-inflate."

Logan swallowed and glanced down to see if the call was still connected.

"What's his prognosis?" Matt asked.

"He'll recover fully, but it will take time. What type of work does he do?"

"He's a photographer." Trevor said.

"That's good. Unless he's one of the ones who hike the Himalayas to get shots, he should be able to continue with his profession once healed. Do you have questions right now?"

Trevor shook his head. "But how do we find you later if we do?"

"Let the nurses know your questions at any time, and I'll find you during rounds."

"Thank you ... for saving him." Matt said.

"As I said before. He's incredibly strong and had a heavy dose of luck." Dr. McKeever smiled. "Must have something good worth fighting for."

Logan stepped away from the group. "Could you hear all that?"

"Yeah. Jesus. I hate to ask, but we really need to field them some questions. I'll try to keep things short, and I'd love to wait till morning, but in situations like this, time is critical."

"I'm sure they'll understand. Clay and I will stay until you get here. And I'll keep trying to reach Rick, Conor, and Calleigh."

"I'm worried, Logan. I've probably called Ethan a hundred times since it happened. What if ... what if Ethan ... He's my everything."

"Hey, one step at a time. Maybe in the chaos he lost his phone, or what if the battery died?"

"Maybe. I ... fuck, I have to go. Please, I'm begging you, tell me the second you hear anything."

"Roger that."

Logan turned and saw that Trevor was on his knees, bent over, and Matt was holding him. He heard Matt's low pitch voice kind of rumble, but he couldn't make out any words. He let the two men share a private moment and looked around for Clay. His husband held out his arms, and Logan walked right into them.

Conor paced the hotel room, glancing at the tele just about every other pass. He, Rick and Calleigh had been in lock down at the hotel since the bombs had gone off. He was going as mad as a box of frogs.

"Con? Come sit with me." Calleigh said.

"I cannae. My babies are out in dat madness an' we are stuck 'ere cause some feckhole in charge tells me I cannae leave!"

Conor jumped and spun towards the door as a loud knock filled the room. He ran over and jerked it open.

"Grapenuts! Holy shoite! Wha' happen to yer? Where yer been?"

Ethan walked past Conor and looked around. "I knocked on all the doors. Just the three of you? No Ryan? No Deshawn? No ... everyone else?"

Calleigh stood and came toward Ethan. "Sit down, Ethan. I can see you're hurt. Let me take a look."

"No! No, I need to go find Ryan and Deshawn. I'm fine. I need the van. I'm ... I'm going to throw up. Excuse me."

Ethan ran for the bathroom, and Conor winced at the sound of him being sick. Ethan didn't look good. His eyes were bloodshot, his clothes torn, and he had dried blood smeared on his face and hands.

"Who are you?" Rick asked.

Conor turned to where Rick stared and found a stranger standing just inside his hotel room door.

"Sorry, I'm Kale. Ethan and I were both near the Federal building when the bomb went off. He said he'd help me get to my family in Pearl City."

"Oh God," Calleigh whispered.

"How near?" Rick asked.

"One block over," Ethan said, as he came out of the bathroom.

Conor took Ethan into his arms. "Yer arsehole. Yer could have been killed."

Calleigh guided Ethan over to the bed. "Have you had any problems with your balance or coordination? Disoriented? Did you lose consciousness? Slurred speech?"

"Umm ... yes?"

Calleigh checked Ethan's head. "You probably have a concussion. I can't tell if you have any skull fractures. We should probably get you to a hospital."

Ethan stood and pushed away from Calleigh. "No! I need to find my husband."

Conor gripped Ethan's shoulders. "Calm yerself. I know yer vexed, but don't take that out on me wife."

Ethan wrapped his arms around his waist. "I'm sorry. I don't know what's wrong with me."

"You've been through a trauma, and you most likely have a head injury. Mood swings are another sign of a concussion." Calleigh took him in her arms. "It's okay. We're all going to get through this."

Conor's vision swam as Ethan broke down and held on to Calleigh. He couldn't even imagine what it was like out there right now, let alone what Ethan must have experienced being so close to one of the bombs.

Everyone spun toward the desk when the room phone rang. Conor dashed over and picked it up.

"Hello?"

"Conor! Thank fuck. Do you know where Ethan is? I can't get a hold of him."

Conor smiled and held the phone out. "'Tis' yer 'usband."

He didn't think he'd ever seen Ethan move so fast, even back in the college days when Grapenuts had been their star striker on the football team.

"Ryan! Oh my God. You promised. You promised you'd tell me, assuming it wasn't some kind of nuke and we were all going to die anyway. But then I was standing there and boom. And I'm flying like fucking Superman. Then nothing and I came to ... And the people. Oh God, the people everywhere. And the smell. And the smoke. And ... and ... where are you? Are you okay? Where's Deshawn?"

Ethan stopped talking and just kept nodding. Conor wanted to put his hand on Ethan's shoulder, but he wasn't sure if the man would accept the touch right then. His friend trembled and shook his head. He dropped the phone.

Conor quickly picked it up. "Ryan? What's happenin'? Ethan's, aboyt ter lose it. Actually, yer man already lost it in me gaff av wax."

"He what? Can you get him to a hospital?"

"Calleigh thinks he's probably got a concussion, but other than dat I think he's just rattled. How aboyt yer?"

"We had a bit of an incident at the headquarters. I can't go into details, but things got a bit fucked up for a while. Give me a sitrep there. Who's there and everyone's status."

"It's only us three, Ethan, an' sum buk who followed him here. Think they ended up in de seem place after. Ryan, yer know where me kids are? Our cell phones are all in SOS mode an' aren't workin' an' de hotel won't let us leave. I tho' we try the landline but believe it or not we didn't know anybody's actual dag an' bone numbers."

"When I talked to Logan, he said Vic and the gang were on their way back to the hotel."

Conor closed his eyes and whispered, *"Go raibh míle maith an Tríonóide naofa iad mo chuid páistí sábháilte."*

He turned to where the rest of the room stood still, watching him. He gave Rick and Calleigh a thumbs up.

"They're gran'. Al' of dem. Should be here soon."

Conor turned his back on his husband and wife because if he looked at them right now he knew he'd never hear the rest of what Ryan needed to tell them.

"What aboyt de three musketeers? An' de deadly duo?"

"They're at Queens Medical Center, and I'm on my way there now. Niall was shot."

"Holy feck! What? How?"

"Long story, but there is a chance it's related to the attack, so that's why I need to question Matt and Trevor."

"Should we go over dere?"

"No, stay where you are. It's best if you stay off the street. When I'm done, I'll come there. Things are moving fast with the intel, and we hopefully will have something actionable soon. I may not be able to stay long, but I need to see Ethan and Deshawn. I need to hold them and see for myself. You know?"

"I know. Me fingers are itchin' ter get ahold of me babies too. I feel loike we've been stuck inside dis feckin' bubble al' day while de world goes nuts around us. I'm glad de three of us were safe an' everythin', but i've felt so trapped yer know?"

"I do. I'll see you soon Con. Let me say goodbye to Ethan?"

Conor held out the phone and Ethan smiled at him.

"Thanks. Sorry I freaked out on you guys."

Conor gave Ethan a pat on the back. "It's gran'. We're al' a wee strung out today."

As soon as Ethan started talking to Ryan, Conor felt his spouses' presence behind him. He turned so he could take both Rick and Calleigh in his arms. Calleigh's gentle cuddles soothed his ragged spirit, while Rick's strong warmth reinforced his determination to see his family through this tragedy in the best way possible.

"The kids should be 'ere soon. Ryan said dat Logan told him they're on de way to de hotel."

"Is everyone okay? Nobody's hurt?" Calleigh asked.

Conor paused. "Ryan didn't say anythin', but I would assume they're al' gran'. He would 'av told us otherwise. Right?"

Rick nodded. "I'm sure. I mean, I know he must be busy, but that's not something you just forget to tell a parent."

"It's done."

Conor had forgotten about Ethan's tagalong until his soft words echoed in the room like a cannon blast.

"Done?"

Kale pointed to the screen. "Look, it's destroyed. It'll never recover from this."

Kale sat on the bed staring at the television. When Conor looked, he saw that the news channel was broadcasting footage taken from a helicopter near the federal building. Smoke poured out of the structure, and the front side of the building facing Halekauwila Street was crumbled in places. Unlike pictures he'd seen of other bombings where the building was flat and it looked as if the front had been sheared off, this building had lots of curves and angles. Almost like they'd built it in sections, then joined them together. So, while some parts appeared untouched, other parts were destroyed. The street itself was fairly narrow, and there was another building directly opposite, which looked to have significant damage too.

"That's where I was." Ethan said, pointing to the screen.

A small grassy area lay about two hundred feet from the section of the building devastated most.

"That was the U.S. District Court." Kale said, pointing to a spot that was little more than a smoldering pile of rubble. "That was my office. If my meeting hadn't been running late, I would have been there." He looked up at Conor. "I would be dead."

He didn't know this young man, but right now that didn't matter. "Well, you're with us now, an' we take care of each other. Yer have family or lads we can git ahold of?"

"My parents live in Pearl City. Before we came here, Ethan and I were going that direction because he said his husband was at the FBI office, but I guess we're staying here now?"

"Ryan, dat Ethan's 'usban', said it was best not ter be movin' around de city. Especially as night falls. Yer can stay wi' us, but we need ter call yisser auld pair. I'm sure they're worried aboyt yer."

The door to the room burst open.

"Pa! Daddy! Momma!"

"*Mo grian, mo gealachí, mo stór!*" Conor kneeled and opened his arms. He almost fell over backwards with the force of his children's' greetings. But he'd gladly suffer a muscle strain compared to the utter rending of his heart had he lost them forever.

Alannah and Brandon ran off to give Rick and Calleigh hugs, but Michael stayed in Conor's arms. He realized his son was shaking, and dampness seeped into his shirt.

"It's gran' *mo grian*. Yisser Pa has yer now. We're together again. Yer just hold on ter me an' I'll protect yer."

He held Michael a little harder, and the little boy winced and stiffened. Conor leaned back and dried Michael's tears with his thumbs.

"What's wrong? Ye hurt?"

Michael lifted his shirt, and Conor saw the bandage that covered his side.

"I got cut. Uncle Vic tried to fix it, but we had to go to the hospital, and they put stitches in me."

He looked carefully at the bandage covering Michael's lower side. He wasn't a doctor or nurse, but it seemed well dressed. Part of him wanted to peek underneath the dressing to see the damage, and part of him was afraid to see the extent of the injury. He'd patched and kissed a lot of boo-boos over the years, but fortunately none of his kids had ever been seriously injured or needed surgery. He felt slightly ill.

Conor clearly needed to talk to Vic, Chase, and Miranda but right now making sure his little moon was feeling safe and secure was more important. He turned to see the rest of the kids sitting on the bed, huddled together like puppies.

"I bet yer al' are starvin'. Why don't yer raid de wee refrigerator an' fend sum snacks. Den we'll put on a movie an' yer can relax."

He must have said the magic words because all six of them rushed past and started calling out what items they wanted. He looked up at Chase, Vic and Miranda who stood just inside the door. Within the last thirty minutes, the room had gone from feeling so isolated to overflowing. He stood and walked over toward his friends.

"Thank yer for takin' care of our laddies an' bringin' dem home ter us. What 'appened ter Michael?"

Chase pulled Conor into a tight hug. "It's good to see you. We were worried because we couldn't get ahold of you by phone."

"Yeah our cells haven't had a signal since it happened. I guess something happened to the tower nearby."

"Michael got cut when there was a pileup on a slide after the bombs went off. It was deep enough that I thought it best to get him seen. They sutured it closed and gave him an antibiotic injection. I also had them give us some pain meds if he needs them. I have to say when we found our way back here around the conference center zone I was very relieved to see the hotel still standing." Vic said.

Conor indicated they should step a little further away from the kids. "How brutal is it out 'dere?"

"Bad. Police and military everywhere. They want everyone off the streets. It wouldn't surprise me if they flew in extra help from the other islands. I heard a few rumors while in the hospital. They're saying casualty numbers from everything are in the thousands. Have you talked to Ryan?"

Conor nodded. "Just got off de dag an' bone with him. Couldn't tell us any details, but said things are movin' quickly. He's comin' 'ere after he gets done interviewin' Matt an' Trevor at de hospital."

"Does anyone else find it strange that Ryan's so involved? I mean, I know he's FBI, but I can't imagine he just showed up and they put him to work?" Miranda asked.

Conor looked over at Ethan, who had his arm around Deshawn, speaking quietly. He looked calmer, but still really beat-up. Probably should suggest he get cleaned up since Conor didn't want the kids to be more scared with Ethan's appearance. Although on the news they'd flashed an alert there was a boil order in effect. Apparently, some of the water treatment facilities had also been attacked. Ethan looked up, and Conor gestured for him to join their small group.

"How's Deshawn?"

"He's doing okay. Scared, but I think we all are. He said his knee feels better with the medicine and brace." Ethan held out his hand for Vic. "Thank you for taking care of him."

Vic pulled Ethan in for a hug. "You look like shit. Do I need to examine you?"

Ethan shook his head. "Calleigh gave me a once over. Most likely a concussion and lots of bruises and scratches, but I'll survive. I'm better off than a lot of others out there."

"Did Ryan say anything to you about what's going on? Why this happened?" Chase asked.

"No, but he's been getting a lot of messages from work while we're here. I know he took a call while we were surfing this morning. The agent in charge of the local field office asked Ryan to come in and consult on something. He couldn't tell me what, but I guess now we know it had something to do with all this."

"But why him? I mean no offense Ethan, but what information could Ryan have that would help them here?"

"I don't know. I don't really care. I just want to see him."

Conor nodded. He understood where his friend was coming from at this point. How had this fun group vacation turned into Niall fighting for his life, Ethan nearly getting blown apart and the rest of them huddled in their hotel room like scared little rats? He looked over at his family. Calleigh had Alannah in her lap. Rick sat between

Michael and Brandon, both boys resting their heads on his chest. He'd never survive if he lost them.

Chapter Ten

♥

R yan stood just outside the hospital room door, watching Matt and Trevor sit beside Niall's bed. Trevor stood and bent over to whisper something in Niall's ear, and his heart monitor beeped, then the number on the screen rose a few points.

"Looks like he enjoyed whatever you had to say," he said as he entered the room.

"How'd you get in here? They're not allowing anyone except one immediate family member per patient on this floor. It took some fancy talk by Matt just to get the two of us in here." Trevor asked.

Ryan whipped out his FBI badge. "Today, this gives me a pass just about anywhere. How's he doing?"

Matt stood and came around the end of the bed. "He's stable. Been in and out of consciousness, but that's normal at this point. It's good to see you, Ry. I heard you had a bit of a close encounter yourself today. Glad to know you're still in one piece."

"That makes two of us."

He'd managed to find a way to get cleaned up after Patterson's assassination. He'd borrowed some clothes from an FBI SWAT officer that made him look ready to kick down doors, but at least he was presentable. Although he still felt the phantom presence of blood and brain matter on his skin.

"I'm sorry to have to do this to you so soon. You must be exhausted since it's late and it's been a fuck of a day. By the way, Logan and Clay are going back to the hotel. Said they'd check in with you in the morning."

Trevor kissed Niall's forehead and came to stand by Matt. "You're still working. Besides, we'll do whatever you need to help catch these fuckers."

Matt put his arm around Trevor. "I'm not sure exactly what information we can give you, though."

Ryan pivoted as a knock echoed through the room and saw Steven and Noelani.

"You'd be surprised what impressions a person can make subconsciously during a trauma. You might know more than you think," she said.

"Matt, Trevor, this is Special Agent in Charge Steven Delgado and Special Agent Noelani Mahi'ai. They're lead on this investigation for the FBI. We're also coordinating information with Homeland Security, NSA and ATF."

Trevor waved. "Hi."

Steven nodded. "I've secured a consultation room so we don't disturb your partner."

Matt looked over at Niall. Ryan could tell that they didn't want to leave. "I promise this won't take long, then you can be with him again."

Matt sighed. "It's okay. I just don't want him to wake up and be scared because he doesn't know what's going on."

Steven led the group to a small conference room down the hall. The room was more of a closet with a round table than anything else.

They all squeezed into a spot, but a few knees knocked together in the process.

Noelani turned on her tablet. "The first thing we need to establish is exactly where you were when the attack happened."

"Do you have a map?" Matt asked.

Noelani spun the screen around and showed them a topographical map of the area. Matt manipulated the image by zooming in and shifting to the quadrant of the island where they'd started the hike.

He turned towards Trevor. "Do you see the ridgeline we were following?"

"Babe, that just looks like a bunch of squiggly lines with varying shades of gray."

Ryan snickered. Trevor was a city boy through and through. He could navigate the streets of Boston and 'The T' with ease, but put him in an area with green fields and he'd become as scared and disoriented as a cat with a whisker pulled. But when Matt and Niall said they wanted a day to go hiking, Trevor had immediately gone out and bought the best hiking boots he could find. That just proved to Ryan how selfless their love truly was.

Matt gave Trevor a kiss, then looked back at the map. Ryan watched as he traced his finger along the map, then stopped. Matt zoomed in on a particular ridge.

"I think we were right about here." He pointed to the screen. "We had made it to the summit of Kōnāhuanui and were working our way towards Manoa Middle. I remember looking up this ridge because the summit was in sight. The plan had been to then go down this direction." He said, his finger hovering over the screen.

Steven whistled. "That's a pretty steep descent. Almost vertical in places. I hope you guys had ropes."

Trevor swallowed. "Seriously?" He looked at Matt. "Is there a little something you forgot to mention?"

"Nope, Niall had faith in you."

Ryan studied the surrounding area of where Matt had shown the attack took place. Infrastructure was absent; the location was a nature reserve.

"What's the link?" He asked.

"Is there one? Or was this just random and we're looking in the wrong direction?" Noelani added.

"No. There has to be something. We don't get random snipers sitting on top of our mountains and especially on a day when half the island is attacked." Steven picked up the tablet and studied it. "I've been on this trail. It's well known within the hiking community of the island, but not very publicized because of the steep terrain and difficulty level. We don't want tourists getting in trouble. At certain points, there are direct lines of sight to metro Oahu. Did the sniper act as a lookout or reporter to inform Kyung once all the attacks were complete?"

"But why shoot at us? I mean, just seeing some guy up on the mountain wouldn't scream out at me, 'hey he's a terrorist keeping watch'," Trevor said.

"Well, clearly he had a weapon. I bet had you come across some guy up on a mountain armed with a rifle that might raise a few eyebrows." Ryan responded.

"Okay, let's go with that. Why be carrying a rifle in the first place?" Steven asked. "Why make yourself so obvious?"

The room went silent. What he knew of Kyung and his associates was that they *did* work clandestinely. It was one reason he'd been so hard to trace over the years. Typically, they had no actionable intelligence of a possible attack before Kyung put a plan into action.

Each time he hit a target, it had been fast, decisive, and then all the players had simply melted into the environment. He didn't utilize suicide bombers, because he didn't want a body or parts of one to be linked back to him. And his supply chain had more twists and turns than a pit full of snakes. He never took credit for anything, unlike other terrorist organizations, who posted on social media platforms the moment something happened. The only reason they'd had any evidence of his involvement in recent years was because there had been an investigation by the CIA.

They'd sent an operative deep undercover within the organization. It had taken two years, after contacting one of Kyung's suspected associates, but he'd finally broken through into the ranks. They'd been slowly building a case against him for connection to the attack on the US Embassy in Chad. That was until a year ago when the operative had gone missing, right about the time Ryan became special agent in charge of the Boston division. Since then, he hadn't kept abreast of the new direction the investigation had taken or the outcome of the missing agent.

"So the four of you were making your way up the ridge. Did you get a look at the shooter at all?" Noelani asked.

"No," Matt said.

Ryan looked at Trevor. He had his eyes closed, then suddenly they popped open, and he gasped.

"Yes! I ... I was looking to the windward side of the island with the binoculars, then whirled. I got a little dizzy looking through the lens, so I focused right on the peak, and I saw a man." He turned towards Matt. "Oh my God, I saw him! Then, it was like a second later, Niall shouted, Holokai was shot, and you were dragging me down." He frowned. "I'm sorry I didn't say anything. I didn't remember until just now."

"It's okay. You've had a lot on your mind. That's why we wanted to sit down with you. Sometimes a simple word or image can jog a witness' memory. How good are those binoculars?"

Trevor scoffed. "Niall bought them. What do you think?"

"Do you think you can give us a description of the man you saw?" Steven asked.

Trevor smiled. "I can do one better."

Holy shit, *if Trevor can lead us to the identity of one of Kyung's men, that will be huge!*

"Matt, where's our stuff? Our backpacks?"

"Probably still in the car, why?"

"Do you remember the day Niall brought those binoculars home? And we were playing with certain features?"

"Yeah ... oh! Shit! You think, it's possible?"

Trevor shrugged

Ryan clenched his fists. He was going to kill them slowly. "What!"

Trevor jumped up. "The item in question is a digital thermal binocular with built-in compass, GPS, altimeter, and ... camera with a human identification range of six hundred meters. It's possible I took a picture of the ridge and caught your suspect accidentally."

"I can't imagine he would know those binoculars take photos. So why take the shot?" Steven said.

"My guess would be simple self-preservation. He noticed a group of people in his immediate vicinity and took aggressive action. Regardless, we need those images. Now." Noelani demanded. "Where do they get stored?"

"On a microSD card."

A knock on the door made Ryan turn quickly. The nurse he'd shown his badge to earlier popped her head in.

"I'm sorry. Dr. Lincoln, Mr. Mitchell but Mr. Roberge is asking for you."

Matt tossed Ryan the keys. "It's in section B-4 of the lot. Blue Jeep Renegade."

Matt and Trevor practically ran from the room as Ryan caught the keys. He looked over at Steven and Noelani. "Let's go."

Ryan paced the office in part to stay awake and in part to keep his mind from lingering over the events of the past twenty-four hours. He'd been working on adrenaline and caffeine, but eventually he knew the stimulants wouldn't be enough and he'd have to get some sleep. He really hoped he'd be able to hold Ethan in his arms when the time came.

The FBI had set up a temporary command center within the National Security Agency's Regional Operations Security Center located outside of Wahiawa, which was about thirty-five minutes north of Honolulu. The NSA people were devouring the images and video stored on the MicroSD card from Niall's binoculars.

Ryan, Steven, and Noelani had been using security footage from the airport to track Kyung's movements from the moment he'd landed. The airport had him until the moment he climbed into a taxi. A call to the company with the license plate and ID number revealed that the cab was not part of their inventory. So that lead was cut off. Ryan had also been monitoring the casualty reports that had been trickling in all morning.

There had been one hundred and eighty people on the Alaska Airlines flight that had detonated on the tarmac. The FAA's preliminary reports showed that a suitcase carrying a bomb had been placed in the cargo hold. Presumably by someone in Kyung's organization. What the investigation was still trying to determine was how the baggage handler had gotten the bomb past all the security check-points then onto the plane. Several FBI agents were sifting through security footage and interviewing airline employees to locate a suspect, but so far hadn't struck gold.

Casualties were greatest at the Convention Center, the site of a girls' volleyball tournament. The number of fatalities and injuries were unclear yet, but preliminary counts based on first responder and hospital records placed the number close to twelve hundred. The only consolation was that the sequential bombs planted throughout the complex had detonated during a break in play.

Fortunately, the remaining six water treatment facilities had taken up the immediate needs for the island, but there was a boil order in effect. It would take time to make repairs to the infrastructure, but the loss of life had been minimal there. Only a handful of employees at each of the three facilities had been affected.

The truck bomb outside the federal building had achieved its objective with deadly accuracy. One hundred and fifty-five were confirmed dead, and hundreds more suffered injuries. His husband being one of them. Which made looking at this event with an objective eye nearly impossible. Just the thought of Ethan lying there, bleeding and unconscious, while insanity reigned around him had Ryan grasping his chest in terror. To make matters worse, he hadn't even verified with his own eyes that Ethan was okay. After Trevor had revealed the evidence on the memory card, Ryan hadn't had the chance to go back to the hotel. Hearing their voices on the phone had helped, but his arms ached to hold Ethan and Deshawn again.

"Ryan! They found it," Steven announced as he and Noelani ran into the room.

Steven held up a flash drive and tossed it to Ryan. Ryan caught it and plugged it into the smart table. He found the file with Steven's directions and opened the image. The image of the jagged green peaks of the Ko'olau Mountain Range filled the large LCD screen.

"Where am I looking?"

Noelani pointed to the top of one peak. "This is the summit of Manoa Middle. That's where your friends said they were headed. And do you see that right there?"

Ryan used his fingers to zoom in on the image, and fuck him running, there *was* a man standing at the top.

"Can we get closer?" he asked.

"Your friend has a seriously cool toy. The resolution on that thing is ridiculous." Noelani said, enviously.

God bless Niall, and his obsession with all things technical and photographic. It wasn't the average hiker who thought to bring state-of-the-art binoculars—complete with digital camera—that could take a crystal clear photo of a snail's slime trail.

"The techs already enlarged and cleaned up the image." Steven tapped on the screen and brought up another file.

Ryan's heart slammed to a halt in his chest, and he choked on the air trapped in his lungs. He nearly started dancing a fucking jig in the middle of the NSA office.

"That's Kyung."

"Holy fuck, you're right." Steven asked.

"That son of a bitch stood overwatch on his own operation. But where the fuck did he go after he shot Niall?"

"Ladies and gentlemen, this is where we come in. Your friend isn't the only one with cool toys."

Ryan turned and saw Agent Disbrow, one of the NSA's finest, whom Steven had introduced him to earlier.

He pointed to the image on the smart table. "Pretty sure you've already shared your toys."

Agent Disbrow scoffed. "That's nothing. My kids' school has one of those things. No ... no ... no. Let's have some real fun."

He slid in between Steven and Ryan, then did some fancy typing with a series of alpha-numeric characters. The screen came to life with a whole other type of menu, and an earth view map appeared. He slid up a digital keypad, then typed in the date and time. The map shifted and rotated until Ryan recognized the island of Oahu.

"Pulled this off a drone video based on the metadata from the image your friend captured of Kyung."

"Holy shit," Noelani said softly. "You guys really are snooping on everyone at all times."

"Well, we prefer to call it monitoring, but yes. We can access information from a variety of sources if deemed critical to national security."

Agent Disbrow hit a button, and Ryan watched one of the world's most wanted terrorists bend to a knee, lift his rifle, fire. The images were so clear; it was like watching a movie. There was no sound, but Ryan imagined he heard the echo of the shot across the mountains. He watched his friends' guide fall; the body going over the edge of the ridge and disappearing into the canopy. Then Niall went down, and while he instinctively wanted to watch Matt and Trevor, Ryan forced himself to focus on Kyung.

"Look, he took off down the other side of the ridge." Ryan said.

"But then he stops." Steven said.

Agent Disbrow zoomed out, and in that moment numerous fireballs shot up into the sky. Kyung stood still, looking through a pair of binoculars like a naturalist while people's lives were being ripped apart by his own design, just a few miles away. Then he started walking.

"Is there a trail that leads out that way?"

Steven frowned. "Yeah, about a dozen. He could have snaked any number of ways down that mountain, and we wouldn't know where he came out with the density of the canopy."

"True. Very true, unless of course you have something like thermal biometric tracking."

Agent Disbrow tapped something on the table, and the footage transformed from a vibrant emerald green to ghostly black and white with a rectangular frame surrounding Kyung.

Steven whistled low and smiled. "Damn, I gotta get me one of these."

"Oh, it's not that hard. Just send the president a text and ask permission to turn on the cable."

"The cable?"

"Yeah, we get all the premium channels."

Ryan smiled even while he advanced the footage several hours, following the locked target down the mountain.

"It looks like he went down the same way your friend described."

"Yeah, and he had a friend waiting for him at the bottom." Agent Disbrow said. He captured a still image of Kyung getting into a car.

Steven accessed the vehicle registration information and frowned.

"What's wrong?" Ryan asked.

"Ikaika Palakiko of Maunawili is the registered owner of that car."

"Driver?" Ryan asked.

"Not likely. Died two months ago from cardiac arrest. A storage lot held the vehicle while his estate went through probate."

"So tracking the car won't do us any good." Ryan looked at Agent Disbrow. "Can you follow him with this thing?"

"Unfortunately no. We'd had this high-altitude drone in operation over the island since we were notified of Kyung's landing, and we were lucky to get this footage. The drone was at the end of its fourteen-day flight time."

"Any other fancy tricks you have hiding up your sleeve? We need to find out where he went. I'm sure he already had plans in place to get off the island. With the airport closed and the water under heavy guard by the Navy, what would be his most likely extraction plan?"

"There are several abandoned and private airstrips on the island. If it were me, I'd have a jet waiting for me." Noelani said.

"True. But we can't stake them all out . And I hate to say this, but what's to say he's even still on the island? This recording is nearly nineteen hours old." Steven said.

"He's here." Ryan announced.

"How are you so sure?" Disbrow asked.

"I spent the better part of four years with this guy on my radar. We don't know a lot, but we do know that he does everything with a purpose. He could have flown in on a private jet and landed on one of those isolated airstrips, but he didn't. No, he flew commercially to the island. Which, let me tell you, how happy that still makes me. He had to know there was a possibility we would see through the fake identity because he did nothing to hide from cameras at the airport, and that would likely lead us to chasing his tail. Then the bombs went off, and since he targeted the airport, he knew the FAA would shut it down. Plus, he's been holing up somewhere on the island with no record of a reservation, rental, or purchase under the same name, or any of his other aliases."

Ryan studied the smart table. Kyung being up on that mountain was the key. His single error was that he did not ensure all the witnesses were eliminated. Also, many around the world had hunted Kyung for the atrocities he'd committed against man for nearly two decades, but now he was trapped on a small island in the Pacific.

"I think we need to look deeper into the one man from his team we have in custody."

"Who?" Agent Disbrow asked. "I was told none of his associates had been captured or identified."

"Patterson." Ryan said.

"But he's dead." Noelani responded.

"And we have his body." Steven answered.

Ryan nodded. "Therefore, he's technically in custody. So let's tear every scrap of information we can get from his home, computers, and cell. Hell, I don't care if they operate by carrier pigeon. I want to know where they get them and interrogate the fucking bird."

Agent Disbrow smiled. "Just give us his profile information and we can tell you what size and style underwear he preferred."

"Let's get to it."

Chapter Eleven

♥

Logan paced back and forth in the hotel room. He hadn't been this agitated for a long time. For some peace, he removed his speech processors and took an extra dose of his anxiety pills. He couldn't shake the feeling that something was still on the horizon. Out of the corner of his eyes he saw Clay's hands moving.

"What?" he signed

"You look anxious. Can I help?"

"No. Thank you. I have that feeling on the back of my neck."

"The same that started the night of the luau?"

"Yes. I can't help but feel this is not over."

*"Don't take this the wrong way, but could that be the PTSD talking?
"*

"I don't know. Maybe."

"Ryan gave us all the information from the investigation. All he was allowed to. He wouldn't let us stay in danger."

"You are right."

Clay crooked his finger at Logan. He walked over to the sofa and sat down. Clay pulled Logan against him. Logan closed his eyes and leaned into Clay's body. Vertebrae by vertebrae and bone by bone, his body relaxed. The cloak of stress and anxiety unzipped. There was nothing like being in his husband's arms. Clay slid his fingers up the back of Logan's neck, massaging the tense muscles, and into his hair. The long fingers sliding along the contour of his scalp did a lot towards soothing the tingles under his skin.

He angled his head to meet Clay's kiss. Their lips touched, then paused, letting the touch linger. He parted his lips, sliding his tongue out to trace the seam of Clay's mouth. As one they opened wider, gliding their tongues together, filling each other's mouths in a dance of passion.

Logan drew away from the kiss. He leaned back so his hands were free to speak. *"Thank you. I needed that. Needed to be reminded, despite the horrors of yesterday, there's still love in the world."*

"I've been in love with you since we were teenagers. No matter the battles we fight in the outside world, our hearts will always be safe."

Logan stood and drew Clay over to the bed. He needed to show Clay just how much Logan understood his words. Logan absorbed the sensations of Clay's skin under his fingertips as he removed each piece of clothing. The tiny sparks zipped along his nerves until reaching his brain to ignite an inferno of hedonistic pleasure. The golden sun shone through the windows of their hotel room. It's brilliant glow a symbol of the happiness he felt in his heart. He placed his hands on Clay's hips, kissed his neck. The vibrations of Clay's moan against his lips resonated from his heart to his cock. He pressed their foreheads together, opening his eyes to meet Clay's. The stormy gray gaze swirled with sensuality.

He turned them and eased Clay down onto the bed. The way Clay cradled Logan's body with his own was a physical manifestation of hearts and souls entwined. He slid a hand up Clay's leg, the fine hairs tickling his palm and exciting the nerves beneath. Blood surged through his veins, singing with life.

His hard cock rubbed against Clay's. Anticipation of sliding inside his husband built with each caress. Their kisses carried with them the vow of unrelenting love, and the desire to nurture each other's growth as they're sling shot through the trials of life. Clay lifted his legs and locked them around Logan's hips. He pushed up to look into Clay's eyes. No spoken or signed language could adequately convey what he observed in them.

Clay captured Logan in his arms, and he became a willing prisoner. Their lips clashed with an urgency that mimicked the need building within them. Logan thrust his tongue deeper, and he rocked their hips together. Logan braced himself on his arms, working his hips so their cocks slid against one another. He opened his eyes when he felt Clay stretching beneath him. The target in sight was the table where they'd stashed their lube. Logan fully supported the objective. Mission achieved, Logan held out his hand, but the cool gel did little to soothe the fire of need that raced through his body. Logan moved to his side, guiding Clay's leg up to rest against his torso. Clay's flesh fluttered against his fingertips.

A vibration of pleasure met his lips as Logan bent down to kiss his husband, whose body opened to his touch. Logan's cock and sac ached and anticipation tightened his muscles, knowing their bodies would soon be together. Clay's breath on Logan's neck had him shivering, while he hissed at the fiery trails that lingered behind Clay's nails as they raked his flesh. Clay's body welcomed Logan's fingers with a heat that rivaled the hottest of deserts. Watching his partner's need rise higher and higher with each massage of his gland built within Logan a source of power that, when unleashed, had the power to reshape their universe, but just as he sensed Clay approaching the edge he backed off.

Clay opened his eyes to meet Logan's gaze. "You evil fucker."

"I love you too."

He repositioned himself between Clay's thighs, then covered his cock with lube. Clay lifted his legs, and Logan accepted the gift, placing Clay's ankles on his shoulders. He aimed his cock at Clay's hole, pressing on the ring of muscle and watching it flare open. Logan closed his eyes to savor the caress of his husband's flesh encircling his as he pushed inside. He gasped at the warm embrace. Clay's tight muscles yielded, and Logan thrust in a slow rhythm.

They coiled their bodies together. Logan smiled as Clay's muscles strained with the effort to pull himself up into a kiss. Out of the million or so they'd shared over the years, this one was the most special. Of course, Logan said that to himself every time. He knew Clay was the other half of his soul. Knew with every beat of his heart that Clay's beat in the same tempo. The hell and uncertainty of the last day did not exist when he was in Clay's arms. He hoped to God that his friends understood just how lucky they all were and took each second to share that with each other.

His heart raced and his blood pounded nearly as hard as he thrust his body into his husband's. Clay's mouth opened in a cry that Logan had no way hearing, but understood all too well. He groaned as Clay's inner muscles clamped around his cock. Clay's hot cum pulsed over his hand, triggering Logan's orgasm. His body pulsed with his release, and he swore his heart nearly burst from his chest. A soft flutter of lips against his chest caught his attention, and Logan looked down to see a prism of love shining from his husband's eyes. He slicked back the strands of Clay's hair that were dampened with sweat. Eventually, Logan found his breath only to have it captured by Clay's mouth. He shifted so their hearts beat against one another, riding a wave of euphoria.

Clay stiffened beside him. He opened his eyes to see Clay's gaze on the door at the other side of the room.

"What?" he voiced, watching Clay's lips for a response.

"There's someone knocking on the door."

They got out of bed and dressed. Clay removed his speech processors from their case and attached them. The second he heard again it was like a part of his brain woke up.

Logan turned and saw that Clay had his service weapon ready as he approached the door.

"Is that really necessary?"

Clay looked at him over his shoulder. "Right now, I'm not taking anything for granted."

"Fair. Just check the peephole before you terrify one of the kids, okay?"

Logan held his breath as Clay did as asked.

"It's Ethan, and he doesn't look happy."

Logan joined Clay at the door as he pulled it open. Ethan walked in and looked around.

"We have a problem. I was watching the news, and they announced that, and I quote, 'A man was brought into Queen's Medical yesterday evening who can identify the terrorist that organized the attack.'"

"What?" Logan exclaimed.

"That's what they said. And then the fucking morons said their source at the hospital reports the man will make a complete recovery."

"They just painted a massive target on Niall, Matt and Trevor's backs. Have you talked to Ryan?"

Ethan looked at Clay as if he were an idiot, and Logan smiled.

"They've been monitoring the networks too, and he's sending some agents to guard Niall and the others. He also said they're working on another angle, but that he couldn't go into any details."

"Well, unlike hospital staff, we can keep our mouths shut. Is there anything he needs us to do?" Logan asked.

"Ryan made it so I could get clearance into the building where they're working. I'm going there now. Can the two of you hang out with Deshawn?"

"Absolutely."

Logan walked over to the windows and looked out toward Waikiki Beach. "It looks so strange being empty like that. In fact, I don't see anyone walking around outside."

"I spoke with the manager, and he said that while the hotel isn't officially on lockdown anymore, they are encouraging guests not to wander around the city until the authorities have contained the situation. Do you think Deshawn might like to go for a swim in the rooftop pool?" Clay asked.

"His knee is still bothering him. We can ask, but he might just want to relax with a movie or something."

"Okay. Go see Ryan and we'll hold down the fort here."

Ethan had lost count of the number of searches the Feds subjected him to and doors escorted through. He blinked as they walked into a large open room filled with massive monitors on the walls. Some showed live news broadcasts and others various types of information. Computer monitors and laptops littered nearly every flat surface, and photos littered the ones without computers. He stopped suddenly as he saw Niall's photo appear on a screen, along with a lot of personal information that his friend probably wouldn't appreciate strangers knowing about him.

"Ethan!"

He spun around at the sound of Ryan's voice. Ethan was surprised he didn't levitate in his effort to get to his husband quicker. Ryan caught him in his arms, and Ethan squeezed with all his strength.

"Oh God, E. I knew you were okay, but I ... I didn't really believe it until just now."

He stared up into Ryan's gaze. It seemed as if Ryan was cataloging every inch of his face, and Ethan traced Ryan's features with his fingers.

"Fuck it," Ryan breathed.

Ethan frowned until Ryan bent his head and captured his lips with his own. There had only been a handful of times in their years together that Ethan swore he could taste the unique flavors of desperation, desire, gratitude and love all at once. Ethan gave every ounce of his own tumultuous emotions back to his husband. Everything around them froze except the thundering beat of their hearts pressed together.

He heard someone clear their throat, and Ethan backed out of their kiss. He turned his head and saw a man standing a couple of feet away watching them while the rest of the room apparently found something on the wall screens fascinating.

"Yes?" he asked.

"I'm sorry. I lost the coin toss and was elected to interrupt you two before clothes started flying."

Ryan took Ethan's hand. "Ethan, meet Agent Disbrow. This is his place."

Ethan took another cursory look around. "Nice. Although it's a bit more industrial than I usually go for."

"Please call me Paul. It's nice to meet you, and I'm sorry for keeping Ryan away while we work through the situation."

"I accepted a long time ago that this is part of him. I can always count on Ryan being there for us when we need him, but sometimes we're together more in thought than body."

He squeezed Ryan's hand and received a smile in return.

"From what I understand, you're quite a busy man yourself. Assistant United States Attorney is no menial job."

Ethan shrugged. "I've been with the Department of Justice since I finished law school as part of the Attorney General's Honors Program. It's been a good place to build a career."

"Ethan, good to see you again," Steven said as he came over. "How's the head?"

"A bit scrambled, but still intact."

"Hmm, well maybe a little scrambling will give you better balance on the surfboard."

He looked at Ryan. "Haven't you ever heard that nobody likes a tattletale?"

Steven snickered.

"I said nothing about how many times you fell off. You just confirmed his suspicions."

"Damn FBI. Always so fucking sneaky."

"I consider that a compliment. Being sneaky has gotten many criminals to cave under interrogation over the years."

Ethan turned his back on Steven. "Have you heard from Trevor or Matt? Are they okay?"

"Yes. One of our agents and an HPD officer arrived and will stay with them until I expressly give him orders not to. We identified the leak at the hospital too. Apparently, one of the night nurses is dating a cameraman from Channel Two. She told him on the phone early this morning, and he ran to the station chief with the exclusive. Which, of course, got picked up by all the national networks and aired for everyone in the world to see."

"Our office has already expressed its displeasure and threatened them with all kinds of federal indictments. They're of course arguing first amendment rights, but I've actually been trying to find a way to use the situation to *our* advantage." Steven said.

Ethan released Ryan's hand. "You mean like using our friends as bait? You're okay with that?"

"Right now it's just talk. Also, you know I'd never actually put them in danger, so we would make sure that Matt, Trevor, and Niall are nowhere near our target area."

"Look, I get it that sting operations garner a lot of success with everyday criminals. But what makes you think this individual or group of individuals would fall for the trap? I mean I don't know any details of who you're dealing with, but based on what I experienced yesterday, this was an extremely well-planned and coordinated attack. And, not that I'm not grateful you let me in here to see Ryan, but should I really be hearing *any* of this?"

Ryan smiled. "Told you."

Paul and Steven both whipped out their wallets, cursing, and handed over some cash to Ryan.

"You're right, Ethan. As much as I like you, this isn't a social hour, and you don't see either my or Paul's spouses sitting over there drinking coffee. What I'm about to tell you doesn't leave this room."

Ethan nodded.

"The name you, and everyone in the world, is trying to discover is Shin Kyung."

He looked at Ryan. "That's why you were called in?"

"Yes."

"So why am I here?"

"Because we believe you have valuable information that can lead us to where Kyung is hiding."

He looked back and forth between Ryan, Paul, and Steven. All three of their expressions were tense, but a predatory gleam also filled their eyes.

"We identified one of the terrorists working with Kyung. His name was Jack Patterson. And he was an FBI agent."

Ethan knew he probably looked a bit like a fish with his mouth gaping and his eyes bugging out. He glanced at Ryan and Steven. Their expressions said everything Ethan needed to know.

"He's dead."

"Yes, assassinated as I walked him out of the building once we'd taken him into custody." Ryan said.

Ryan had his fists clenched and that telltale tick in his jaw. He was pissed. But whether it was because one of his own had turned traitor, or because that traitor was dead and unable to serve for his crimes, was debatable.

"When *you* walked him out?"

Ryan sighed. "Yeah, E. He took a round to the head from a sniper. And yes, I was too close for comfort, and no, I couldn't tell you, and yes, I'm sorry."

Ethan wrapped his arms around Ryan and held him. He could have lost him. His stomach turned, and his heart ached. Had he been just fractionally closer to the Federal building or had Ryan been in a slightly different position, Deshawn could have lost one or both of his new parents. That little boy had been through enough pain and turmoil in his life. It was his and Ryan's responsibility to protect him now.

Is it time to make some changes in our lives? But how can I ask Ryan to give up—

"This was after Patterson set off a bomb in the FBI headquarters that effectively had everyone scrambling while he downloaded several terabytes of secure data." Steven said.

Ethan pushed away from Ryan, every muscle in his body contracting.

"You were in a building that *exploded* too?"

"It's not like I planned on this, E."

He pinched the bridge of his nose. "I know. I know. I'm sorry. It's not you I'm pissed off at."

Paul interrupted, "Not that I'm trying to get in the middle of a marital thing here, but if it makes you feel any better, it was only a little bomb. Nothing like the Federal building or convention center. As Steven said, designed to serve more as a distraction than destruction."

Ethan let out a long breath, counted to five and hit reset. "Okay. So I'm going to ask again, why am I here?"

"Because we've shredded Patterson's life apart and confirmed what we at the Bureau suspected for a long time." Steven said.

Ethan waited, but Steven just stood there. "Well?" He exclaimed.

"The man was a world-class idiot. He broke the cardinal rule of any terrorist organization."

What the fuck was Steven talking about? Ethan had a splitting headache, he felt every bruise on his body, and he hadn't had a decent cup of coffee in two days. He thought about what Steven wasn't saying, then smiled.

"Don't talk about the terrorist organization?"

"Exactly! See, I told you he'd get it," Steven said.

Ryan placed his hand on Ethan's lower back, and he winced. "Sorry, Ry. Not you. Think I landed on something when I got blown backward yesterday."

Ryan frowned. "Have you seen a doctor?"

Ethan smiled. "Yes. Two actually. And two nurses. As well as an Irish busybody. I'm fine. Just banged up. So Patterson was in contact with someone else from Kyung's organization?"

Paul made a few keystrokes on a wireless keyboard, and one of the large monitors next to them changed to a screen that looked like a bunch of weird code to Ethan.

"Patterson used a secure file transfer protocol to transfer data from the FBI server to a remote system. The NSA backtracked the transfer once we hacked Patterson's security network. It wasn't that hard for our people, but based on what Steven said, it was way above Patterson's capabilities."

"So someone set up the system for him, and he just hit the green button, so to speak?"

"Yes."

"And let me guess, you know who set it up?"

Paul smiled. "We do now." He hit another key, and the image on the monitor changed.

"That's Kale!"

"That's the name he gave you?" Paul asked.

"Yes, Kale Palakiko. I met him yesterday just after the attack on the Federal building. He's Judge Wilson's assistant in the District Court."

"His real name is actually Hyuk Ch'oe. He's North Korean, and the US granted him asylum seven years ago. He's been living on the island for six months. Until now we've had no reason to monitor his activities."

"So he's not an attorney?" Ethan asked.

"No, there is no Judge Wilson in the U.S. District Court of Hawaii. Hyuk has been working as a driver for a local seafood market on the island."

"Then why...?"

"We believe he was serving as a spotter during the attack on the Federal building. Most likely, he reported to Kyung when the mission was completed. Did you see any devices on him? He may have even been the person who set the bombs, but we haven't proven that yet."

Ethan was going to be sick. He'd talked to Kale, no Hyuk. He'd believed his story. The young man had seemed so genuine. So terrified.

"Holy shit! I took him back to the hotel. I introduced him to our friends and our kids." He was going to faint. "I told him my husband works for the FBI," he whispered.

Ryan gripped Ethan's shoulder. "Breathe Ethan. It's going to be okay. Is he still there?"

He shook his head.

"On my way here, I dropped him off at a house in Pearl City. He ... he said it belonged to his parents."

"Do you remember the address?" Paul asked.

He closed his eyes and tried to calm his mind. He had to stop freaking out and think clearly. Ryan and the agents needed the information so they could catch the sons of bitches who'd attacked the island. He took out his phone and flipped to Google Maps. Then handed it to Paul.

"He said he'd give me directions to avoid the areas that were still closed because of the bombs. It felt like we drove in circles, but eventually stopped there. Then, I used my GPS to get here. When I asked him for his number, he gave me some excuse about his phone getting damaged yesterday." Ethan frowned. "However, now that I think about it, immediately after the bomb went off I asked him if he had a phone and he said yes, but the battery had died. I just wanted to check on him before we went home."

Paul quickly brought the information onto the screen. "The information says that someone purchased the house as a foreclosure with cash in January of last year. The deed is in the name of Rebecca Shinagawa. Who has no other presence on the island, but paid her taxes last year and has monthly utilities."

Ryan rubbed Ethan's back as he studied the screen. "I don't suppose you can get one of your fancy drones to check out the house?"

"Since it's a private residence, and we only have circumstantial information, I won't get authorization for a fly-by. Unfortunately, we're going to have to go old school and knock on the door."

He looked at Ryan. "You're going, aren't you?"

Ryan led Ethan away a few steps. "I have to, E. There's a chance that Kyung is at that house."

"What about our friends? Kale or Hyuk or whoever he is, knows where they are. He knows about you. What's to say that he won't come back and use them as hostages or something?"

"I keep telling you that you watch too many crime dramas. Mostly in situations like that, the terrorists are going to hide out until the heat calms down, then slink away. Unless they are forced into a corner.

"Oh, you mean like a situation where you raid their hideout?"

"First, there will be no raid unless we actually determine they are present, and then at that point we will not let them waltz out the door for a day trip to Waikiki."

Ethan heard the logic in Ryan's argument, but he knew how sometimes things did not go according to plan. And he still felt guilty for exposing his friends and their kids, as well as his own, to a terrorist.

"I hear you, but I would feel better when I go back to the hotel, we at least move rooms or something."

Ryan nodded. "That's smart. I'll notify the hotel and have them make arrangements. There's got to be somewhere you all can go."

Ethan pulled Ryan down for a kiss, and if it lasted longer and got a little more heated than general public displays tolerated, the NSA employees could kiss his ass.

"You come back to me, Ryan Ashton."

"I'll see you soon."

"Ryan, it's time to go," Steven yelled

Ethan felt a presence behind him and turned to see another agent looking at him expectantly.

"Mr. Harrison, if you follow me, I'll take you to be debriefed. Then you can be on your way."

He nodded. Hopefully, this wouldn't take long.

Chapter Twelve

♥

Ryan checked his weapon one last time as Steven pulled up to the house. The building, in a middle-class neighborhood, appeared unremarkable.

"There's one car in the carport. I wonder if he has any sugar we can borrow." Ryan said.

"I sense a bit of sarcasm in your tone. Remember, we're just paying a visit. We have no proof that Kyung is inside. We only know for sure that Ethan dropped Ch'oe at this location, but a woman owns the house.

"A woman who is a phantom."

"Maybe, but I seriously doubt one of the world's top ten terrorists is going to open the door and invite us in for a cup of coffee. For all we know, this location was just a staging area or might even be a decoy."

Ryan patted his concealed tactical vest. He wasn't taking any chances. "Maybe, but maybe we scrounged up enough luck to actually locate the viper's nest. The agents sitting on Ch'oe's apartment still checking in?"

"Yes. No activity."

Ryan tapped his deep-insertion earpiece. "Paul and Noelani, are you in position?"

"Ready to go. If you spot Kyung or Ch'oe, just say the magic words and we'll have this place surrounded." Paul said.

Paul and Noelani took up a position a block away. A SWAT team stood by. Of course they didn't want to give away their intentions just yet, so the first order of business was to establish contact with someone in the house.

"You ready?" he asked Steven?

"Always. And you can't tell me a part of you doesn't miss the rush of knocking on doors a little bit."

"I'm not the one who was dancing in his seat on the way over here?"

They got out of the car. Ryan looked at the house and let out a long breath. Maybe he did miss the action of being a field agent a little, but he also knew at forty-four his body didn't handle stress as efficiently as when he was younger.

He walked towards the gate, keeping an eye out around the area. The chain-link fence surrounding the property rattled as he pushed open the gate. He detected no movement behind the curtains, and while he really hoped this would be a clean and easy arrest, he also had enough experience to know that a man like Kyung was not the type to simply let himself get arrested.

Steven knocked on the front door, and Ryan tensed inwardly while trying to appear relaxed on the outside. The door opened, and Ryan came face to face with a young woman.

"Can I help you?"

Steven smiled. "Yes, Ma'am. Are you Rebecca Shinagawa?"

"Yes," she said tentatively.

"Excellent, we're with the FBI. I'm Special Agent Delgado, and this is Special Agent Ashton. We had your name listed as a possible missing person after the attacks yesterday. You work as an event manager at the convention center, correct?"

Ryan saw the barest hesitation in the woman's eyes. She was likely trying to play out the odds of what would work in her favor. To go along with the story they'd concocted, or correct them with some other story. Years of working interrogations had him studying her microexpressions, and Ryan knew they'd hit pay dirt. He didn't know who this woman was, but she was not Rebecca Shinagawa.

"Yes, that's right."

Steven sighed a bit too dramatically in Ryan's opinion

"Great! I'm glad to see that you're fine. There must have been some kind of confusion."

"Yes, well, I can understand that given all that happened. I actually called in sick to work yesterday."

Ryan shifted his position so he could see inside better, but the woman closed the door a fraction more. "Maybe you can help us with some of your co-workers who are also on our list. Do you know Kale Palakiko?"

"No, I'm sorry, I don't know that name."

"Oh, that's interesting. He's listed as living at this address too. How about Hyuk Ch'oe?"

She was clearly mentally scrambling, and Ryan smiled.

Busted

He detected movement behind the woman, and Ryan grabbed his weapon. "Gun!"

Steven kicked in the door, and Ryan entered. "FBI, don't move."

He ducked as a man and the woman ran towards the kitchen to the right, firing a barrage of bullets at them as they went.

"They never listen, do they?" Steven asked while he braced against the wall next to a large casement opening.

"I guess they don't teach manners at terrorist school." He said from his crouch behind the only piece of furniture in the room. Ryan peered out and let out a quick breath.

Yippee, no new orifices.

He gestured silently to Steven that he was headed toward the kitchen, and Steven let him know he was going through the opening into what looked like an eating area.

As soon as he came around the wall, he saw the woman on the floor, who hadn't been so lucky, and now had a neat hole in the center of her forehead and several in her torso.

"Shit." Steven cursed. "Paul, Noelani, shots fired, and a confirmed dead woman. Send in SWAT."

"Already surrounding the house and we're located behind the property in case you get a runner."

Ryan stepped through a doorway and found himself in the room Steven had just cleared. There was no furniture. No décor. But three doorways punctuated his view. How had the shooter gotten past them? He crossed the room and headed for the door to the far right.

"Clear," he announced.

He heard Steven say the same, both through the earpiece and through the wall separating him from the room next door. They met each other and, as a team, proceeded toward the next room.

"Shit!" he yelled as more bullets aimed for his face. He braced his back against the doorframe, and Steven did the same opposite him. "This is the FBI. Slide your weapon to us and come out. I'm not in the mood to kill anyone today."

'Liar' Steven mouthed, and Ryan shrugged. What the terrorists didn't know would kill them. He gestured he would go high and Steven low. Then, using his fingers, he counted down.

He swung his body around and found a small bedroom. One window was open, but no bad guy in sight.

"Be advised, we lost one unidentified subject through a window in the property's rear."

Ryan wasn't taking anything for granted. He was about to peek through the window when the glass shattered inward. He ducked and saw a bullet hole in the wall opposite him.

"SWAT commander Reilson here, we've taken him into custody. Be advised he is not, I repeat, *not*, the primary target."

"Is it Ch'oe?" Ryan asked.

"Negative. Says his name is Haywood Chablowme. I assume he thinks us SWAT folk have a sense of humor."

"Fuck," Steven said. "Let's go."

The house contained five bedrooms and two baths, yet they met no further resistance.

"Clear," Ryan announced as they walked out of the last bedroom.

"No basement, no attic. Looks like he wasn't here." Steven said.

Ryan paused. He still felt a tangible pull from the unfinished scene. Their window diver could not possibly be the man who shot at them in the living room. So unless he became a ghost and disappeared, he had to be in the house somewhere.

He put his finger to his lips, and Steven nodded. Ryan examined the room again, looking for something. He backtracked through each room they'd cleared, giving it the same treatment with no success. The rooms were all bare, closets all empty. It appeared they had not found the nest at all, but just a hollow tree the snakes had hidden in.

He made it back to the kitchen, but came to an abrupt stop.

"What?" Steven asked.

"Does something about this room look wrong to you?"

"You mean besides the dead person on the floor?"

Ryan walked around the woman's body. "She took one round to the head and two to the chest, but where's all the blood?"

"It's ... hmm ... that is weird."

"Do you have gloves?"

Steven whipped out a pair of black latex gloves and handed them over. Ryan slid them on and gently tilted the woman's body up.

"Look at this floor."

"Well, I'll be a sonofabitch. We probably never would have noticed it if she hadn't fallen over the hatch."

The woman had fallen directly on top of a secret trapdoor. The only reason the edges were obvious was because of the awkward blood pattern. No hinges were apparent. Ryan pressed on the floor with his foot, but nothing happened.

"Damn, where's my crowbar when I need it?" Steven asked.

Then he noticed a light switch on the side of the base cabinet. "Weird spot." He flipped the switch, and there was a click.

"I'll be fucked." Steven whispered.

Ryan held his weapon ready and gestured to Steven to get the door. He held up his fingers and counted down from three. Steven lifted the door. Ryan let out a breath as it opened without a noise. Beneath the kitchen was access to the crawl space. There was a good chance that as soon as he stuck his head through this hatch, he could lose it.

Steven signaled for him to wait. He took out his cell phone and turned on the front-facing camera. Steven stuck it through the opening, and Ryan watched the screen.

He shook his head. "It's too dark."

"SWAT rover?"

"We don't have time. We're going to have to drop our balls and go through."

"Now I remember why I enjoy being in charge."

Ryan nodded and took half a second to pray he wasn't making the worst mistake of his life. Steven handed him a flashlight that he'd had on his keychain.

Guess these little things do come in handy.

He jumped through the opening and quickly assessed the area, pivoting right and left, but there was no ghost in the darkness or international terrorist waiting to kill him with a Sterling submachine gun.

"Clear."

Steven came down through the hatch. "Why have a secret trapdoor if you're not going to hide under it?"

Ryan swung his light around and saw a pile of dirt in the corner. He shuffled over there to get a better look. "So you can dig underneath it. He's gone full *Great Escape* on us."

"Ok I am not a groundhog. This is where we call in some help to find out where this thing goes."

"Goddamn it. He was here. I know it, and we fucking lost him."

"For the moment, but now he's on the defensive. Something Kyung has never been before. Let's get the evidence response team in here. Maybe we can at least lift his prints off something."

"Ryan, you need to get out here. We found a back shed full of intel, and our window-jumping friend just gave some information you're going to want to hear," Paul said through the earpiece.

He shuffled over to the lattice panel that surrounded the crawl space. He gave it a solid kick, then crawled out into the backyard.

Steven came out behind him. "That was efficient. Where's Paul?"

"Over here. Our guest has some information he wants to impart in exchange for the death penalty."

Ryan looked the unknown man up and down. Late twenties. Long hair. Asian. And wearing a smirk he'd love to smack off. "Oh yeah? It had better be pretty damn good."

"It's your friends who are serving the death penalty. And their sentence is about to be carried out."

Matt handed off a cup of coffee to the guard outside Niall's door. "I hope black is okay."

"Thank you, Sir. I've grown to tolerate black since we don't exactly have an expresso machine at HPD."

Matt smiled. He knew he was spoiled since he did in fact have such a machine in his office back home. He pushed the door open, holding two more cups of coffee.

"How is our patient today?" he asked

Trevor jumped up and took a coffee from Matt. "He's being whiny. I mean, I don't understand what the big deal is about having a plastic tube sticking out of your chest."

Matt glanced at Niall and took a sip of coffee.

"And now you're standing there drinking the very thing I crave and am forbidden to have."

He walked over to the bed and leaned down to press his lips against Niall's. Each kiss they'd shared since Niall had woken up early that morning had brought a level of pleasure he'd never experienced. Most likely because they'd almost lost Niall, and his heart rejoiced in the experience of renewing their connection.

Matt slipped his coffee-coated tongue into Niall's mouth, and their shared groans had him wishing they could share more than a kiss.

"Better?" he asked after he pulled away, albeit reluctantly.

"A little. It would make me feel incredibly better if I could watch you fuck Trevor."

Matt whipped his head around as Trevor started coughing.

"Oh ... oh God. Coffee up the nose. Not. Good." Trevor sputtered.

Matt smiled. "If you're a very good boy and do as your doctors say without complaint, I'll see what I can arrange."

Matt glanced up as Niall's heart monitor spiked several points. He smiled and cupped the side of Niall's face. Had they lost this man, he and Trevor would have gone on. He knew it was possible, but their souls would never have been the same.

"Sei la mia anima gemella"

Trevor picked up Niall's other hand. "I many not have Matt's way with fancy words, but I've been thinking all morning about how ... When I look into your eyes I can see you traveled a great journey to find your way home to us, and I promise to never take that for granted."

Niall squeezed both Matt and Trevor's hands. "As I said when we first found each other, our souls are bound. *Manto* instructed should one of us become lost, he must look within himself for the pathway home. As long as there is breath within my body, my path will always lead back to you."

Matt knew Niall believed his words to the very core of his being. And that absolute certainty was the only thing that had kept him going yesterday and throughout the long night. Niall would be in the hospital another week, and the doctors already forbid him to fly for another three. So their stay in Hawaii was extended, but they would work things out.

"Now, will one of you going to explain to me what happened and why there is a policeman as well as a man in a suit hovering outside my door?"

Trevor sat in the chair beside the bed and tentatively took another sip of coffee. He looked up at Matt, and he knew that was Trevor's way of asking him to explain.

"Yesterday, there was a coordinated terrorist attack on the island. Since we've been here with you, all we know comes from the news reports that have aired continuously since it happened. Ryan is part of the investigation, and apparently they think that the man who shot you might have something to do with what happened."

Trevor set his cup down on the small table beside Niall's bed. "I was using your binoculars when the shots went off. They confiscated the binoculars, hoping I had photographed the sniper on the ridge."

Niall tried to sit up, but winced and fell back onto the pillows. "You … you say there was an attack? Is everyone else okay?"

Matt nodded. "It took a while, but we talked to the others. A few bumps, bruises, and close calls, but you're the only one with holes in them."

"Well, except for Michael. But that was more of a really bad cut than an actual hole." Trevor said. "Everyone is back at the hotel, except for Ryan. He's doing his FBI thing."

"And the reason for the guard?" Niall asked.

Matt rubbed the back of his neck. "Precaution really. It seems a night-duty nurse ran her mouth and the news stations started reporting that you could identify the terrorist."

"But that's not accurate." Niall said.

Trevor nodded. "But the bad guys don't know that. So, until Ryan catches the fucker, we have a chaperone."

A knock on the door had Matt standing. He knew in reality that a terrorist wouldn't knock and politely ask to enter the room, but it didn't change his protective instincts. He relaxed when Niall's doctor stepped in.

"Hello Mr. Roberge. I'm Dr. Nelson. Not sure if you remember me from last night. You were still a bit out of it."

"Hello, I think I have a vague memory of you bending over me."

Trevor snickered, and Matt shot him a look. Trever mouthed, "What?" and Matt couldn't help but roll his eyes. He saw Niall's eyes shift towards Trevor, and their partner had a little side grin.

"Please excuse Trevor. He's sleep-deprived and over-caffeinated. Therefore, his inner tween has emerged." Niall said.

Dr. Nelson smiled. "It's fine. I sort of walked right into that one. I can assure you, your partners have handled themselves admirably. How are you feeling?"

"A bit like a sieve, but it's a little easier to breathe than earlier this morning."

"That's good. How are your pain levels?"

"More than smacking my thumb with the hammer, less than getting bitten by a shark?"

"Okay. I've instructed the nurses to maintain your pain medication levels, but we'll slowly wean you off over the next several days."

"How long does my tentacle need to stay in?"

"Until we're sure all the blood and air that was surrounding your lungs is gone. Probably another couple of days. Let me check your incision. Do you want your partners to step out?"

"No."

Dr. Nelson nodded and pulled down Niall's gown. He removed the dressing, and Matt swallowed hard as the long, angry-looking scar appeared. Trevor came around the bed and stood beside him. He gripped Trevor's hand.

"Oh my God," Trevor whispered.

Matt squeezed and leaned down to say softly, "It's okay, *Bello*."

Trevor nodded. "Just gives us more scars to kiss, right?"

Niall's torso had turned into a map of his history. Matt's gaze landed on every piece of Niall's story. The scars from his attack as a young man, the gunshot wound, and the fresh scar where the doctors had had to crack his chest open.

"Things appear to be healing well, Niall. I'll let the nurses know that when you feel up to it, they can arrange a light meal. Maybe something with protein."

Matt covered Trevor's mouth with his hand.

Dr. Nelson turned and faced Matt and Trevor. "The two of you need to go get some sleep. Go back to your hotel, eat a healthy meal and don't come back for at least six hours. I would say twenty-four, but I figure there's no way that will happen."

"Don't worry, doc, I'll make sure they follow your orders," Niall said.

Dr. Nelson nodded and left the room.

Niall crooked his finger at Trevor. "You are incorrigible."

Trevor sat on the edge of the bed. "I don't know what you could possibly mean."

Niall gently pulled on Trevor's hand and he leaned in to place them on either side of Niall's head.

"When I get to where taking a breath doesn't feel like the fires of hell are racing through my chest, then I promise I'll make every one of those dirty thoughts of yours come true. Until then, I'm putting Matt in charge of your punishment."

Trevor smiled. "I don't think that will be a deterrent. Matt's punishments usually lead to me to screaming in pleasure."

Matt snuck up behind Trevor and whispered in his ear, "You have no idea what my true abilities are, *Bello*. I can leave you on the edge for so long your body will convince your brain it's torture. And just when you're about to reach the breaking point, I'll call Niall. He'll be the one to decide if I bring you relief or deny you the release you crave."

He placed the tiniest of kisses on the back of Trevor's neck and smiled as his lover's body trembled. Letting his darker side out to play every once in a while was such fun.

"Come along. It's time we let Niall get some rest."

Trevor took his time giving Niall a kiss goodbye, and the sight made Matt's heart happy. He slipped in and they shared a three-way kiss for a few moments. He could tell when Niall's body signaled that he needed rest, and he guided Trevor back.

"Sleep well, *Caro*," he said softly.

Matt took Trevor's hand and led him from the room. He and Trevor hadn't left the hospital since bringing Niall into the emergency room. The first order of business when they got to the hotel was a shower.

"Hey, where's our chaperones?" Trevor asked.

Matt jerked his head up and looked to either side of the door. Sure enough, Officer Iona was gone.

"I don't know. Wait here. I'm going to find a nurse and see if they know anything."

Matt walked toward the nurses' station. Maybe the police officer had just stepped away to use the restroom? He saw Michelle, one of Niall's nurses, at the desk.

"Excuse me, have you seen the guard for Niall's room?"

Michelle looked up from the computer and frowned. "No. I'm sorry, I just came out of another patient's room."

"It's okay. I know you're busy. We were about to go back to our hotel to get cleaned up and rest, but I don't feel comfortable leaving Niall vulnerable. I'll check the restroom; maybe he just needed a break."

Matt understood that nature sometimes called, but he would have expected to see agent Donaldson covering the door. The men's bathroom was located down the opposite hall. Matt gestured he was heading in that direction to Trevor, who waited beside Niall's door. Trevor nodded. Matt smiled at how his lover—whose frame took up less than half of the doorway—stood as stiff as one of the Queen of England's Guards.

He pushed open the door to the restroom. "Officer Iona?"

Silence echoed. Nobody stood at the urinals or by the sinks. Matt sighed, then stooped to peek at the floor beneath the stalls. He saw feet.

Well shit! I guess that's literally the case here.

"I'm sorry to disturb you, but has there been anyone else in here in the last couple of minutes?"

Matt frowned when there was no answer from the occupant. This was awkward, but he needed to get some answers before he raised any alarms.

"I'm not trying to be rude, but can you answer me? I'm looking for an on-duty police officer."

There was still no response from the stall, and now the back of his neck tingled. He knocked on the door, but instead of the door remaining firm, it swung inward.

"Fuck!"

Matt bolted out of the bathroom and immediately heard shouting coming from the end of the hall. He sprinted back toward Niall's room and slid to a halt when he saw Trevor fighting with a man wearing a doctor's coat.

"Hey!" he shouted.

"Matt! He's not a real doctor. He ... Ow you fucker!" Trevor kneed the man in the groin then landed a wicked right cross.

Matt picked the man up off the floor and held him tight against his body. "Who are you? What are you doing here?"

"Let me go! My name is Dr. Palakiko. I have some medication for this patient."

Matt didn't recognize the man, and Dr. Nelson had said nothing about a new order for Niall. As he was about to loosen his hold, he looked at Trevor. Trevor's left eye was already turning black and he was hunched over like he'd taken a hard hit to the ribs.

Why would a doctor engage in a fistfight with a hospital visitor, and where is the rest of the staff?

"Show me some hospital identification and tell me what medication you planned to administer."

Trevor started rooting around in the lab coat. "No ID tag, but I found these."

Matt peered at the vial of potassium chloride and a capped syringe. There was no way in hell that was legit.

"Trevor? Matt? What's going on out there?" Niall yelled from inside the room.

"Go in there, call security, and then call Ryan."

As soon as Trevor disappeared through the door, Matt slammed his captive against the wall. "Who sent you?"

"My name is—"

"I don't give a shit what name you call yourself. I want to know who sent you. Why are you trying to kill this man, because there is no other reason for you to have that vial?"

Matt pushed a little harder against the man pinned to the wall. He felt the tension in his body and pulled back on his hands a little harder.

"You're going to break my arms!"

"Answer the question!"

"Dr. Lincoln, what is going on here?" Michelle shouted.

"This man is impersonating a doctor, killed officer Iona, and was trying to poison Niall with a lethal dose of potassium chloride. Trevor has called security, but I want to know who sent him."

When his captive turned his head and their eyes met, Matt realized this person had no intention of giving up his secrets. He had also never seen such a dead pair of eyes in all his years of psychiatry.

He heard running feet and angled his body so he could maintain his grip but look over his shoulder. A security guard, agent Donaldson, two cops and Ryan headed in their direction.

"I bet they have much more effective ways of making you talk." He said as he lifted Palakiko up to turn him around.

Palakiko thrust his head back and slammed his skull against Matt's nose.

"Son-of-a-bitch!" Matt screamed.

"Matt!" Trevor shouted as he ran from Niall's room

"Hyuk Ch'oe, freeze!"

Matt kneeled on the floor, his head spinning from the slam. Through blurry vision, he saw the police tackle the man who'd killed one of their own. His body flopped on the ground like a fish out of water.

"Looks like they got him with a Taser," Trevor said while kneeling down next to Matt. "What did they call him?"

All the commotion of the last several minutes had garnered them a whole circle of onlookers.

"I don't know. But I have a feeling they know something we don't."

"Ch'oe, you're under arrest for conspiracy to use a weapon of mass destruction, resulting in death."

Matt turned towards Trevor as Ryan continued to rattle off a list of charges.

"Apparently they know a lot of somethings we don't."

Chapter Thirteen

"Where are we?"

Ryan sat across from Ch'oe, waiting for his captive's next move in this chess game of an interrogation.

"What do you want? This is not a police station."

"Nope."

"Then what are we doing here? You said I was under arrest."

Ryan looked around the abandoned seismograph station. The roof was partially missing, and the jungle had invaded the concrete walls. Noelani also said that people believed the place was haunted.

"Oh, don't worry. You're going away for a very long time. Smile." He snapped a photo, then scrutinized his phone before he menaced, "Or I could just execute you here and claim it was an accident. I guess we'll just have to see."

"Why did you take a picture of me?"

Ryan shrugged. "Souvenir. Oh, and I was just sending my husband a text."

Ch'oe scowled.

"What's wrong? You remember my husband, don't you?" Ryan's phone pinged, and he smiled. "He remembers you." Another alert went off, and Ryan glanced down, then chuckled at the extremely rude bitmoji Ethan had sent. He turned the phone around so Ch'oe could see the screen. "And he sent you a gift."

"It's too bad that fag wasn't closer when those bombs went off."

Ryan stood, walked over to the wall. He picked up an old piece of rebar and studied it for a moment. It was pleasingly substantial. The ridges dug into the skin of his palm as he gripped it tightly. He took a couple of steps backward, then spun and swung the iron bar with all his might.

Hyuk screamed and doubled over. The reinforced steel had most likely broken a couple of ribs and had caused a gash to Ch'oe's left arm. He tried to get out of the chair that Ryan had cuffed him to. He stood nearby and twirled the bar. The isolated area around the building ensured no locals or tourists would hear Hyuk's screams. Ryan stood in the corner and watched until he'd had enough.

"Would you shut up? Nobody is out there. Now here's the thing, we're going to sit down and have a little chat. Then, if I like what I hear, I'll call off the drone strike that is scheduled in the next ten minutes."

"You can't do this! You have rules to follow about prisoners."

Ryan's laugh even sounded evil to his own ears. "You blew up half this island. I have the authority to do whatever I want."

"I need a doctor. You broke my fucking arm!"

"Maybe. You killed nearly fifteen hundred people and caused hundreds of millions in damage. So, gotta say I'm not in that big of a rush to get you help. I'm actually pretty disappointed in you. I mean either the pickings are really slim here in the Pacific or Kyung has lowered his standards on who he works with. I mean, not only did you not fulfill the mission he sent you on, but you got caught, and you still had evidence on you that led us right to your boss."

That was a partial bluff, but the man didn't need to know that. The question was, would he fall for the bait?

"You're lying." Ch'oe said with a slight wheeze.

"Am I? You remember telling Ethan right after the attack that your phone battery died, right. Well you ... lied. In more ways than one. Not only was your phone working, but you used it to send a text. Now, any self-respecting terrorist would have ditched the phone they'd used by now, but not you. And do you know why?"

"I'm sure you're going to tell me why you think so."

"That phone contained the security key information for a remote server. The same server that received the file transfer data from the FBI field office. And it was you who set up the transfer. It was also you who then sent that security key to Shin Kyung."

"I'm sorry, who? I don't know anyone by that name."

Ryan laughed. "Oh, you think I'm looking for a confession. No, no, I don't need you to confirm anything. We've got what we need from your little not so secret bat cave. Just out of curiosity, whose idea was it to keep all the plans, list of sleeper cell members and physical evidence of the bombs all stored in that shed?"

"What shed it that?"

"The one that has your fingerprints and handwritten notes plastered everywhere."

"If you have all this information, why am I sitting here rather than in prison?"

"Well, maybe you're not as high in Kyung's operation as you'd like to think. Because if you were, then you'd know he doesn't leave loose ends. And you, my friend, are a *huge* loose end."

Ryan let that sink in, and he saw the moment Ch'oe made the connection in his brain. He walked over to the steel door and turned the lever. The sound of metal grating on metal hurt his ears, but he was betting good old Hyuk was moments away from pissing his pants.

"Where are you going?"

"I have a date with a sea turtle. Have a nice life. Although I've already placed my bets that it won't be a long one."

"You can't leave me in here like this," Hyuk shouted

Ryan waved as he pulled the door shut.

"Hey!"

"Don't worry. I texted your boss from your phone right after we got here. I'm sure he'll be here soon to deal with you." He shouted through the door.

As he walked away from the cinderblock building, he heard Hyuk's screams. Ryan headed into the jungle, and just as the vines covered him, Hyuk's shouts stopped.

Guess that little transdermal sedative did its job.

"I'm clear. Is everyone in position?"

"Roger. You think this will actually work?" Steven said over the earpiece.

"This is Paul. Our drone has spotted movement closing in on your location. There's a truck moving fast up the road. Once you confirm Kyung is onsite, we're moving in."

"Your guys are good. I feel totally alone in this jungle."

Ryan crawled into a dead log and waited. He wanted to see the man who'd orchestrated one of the worst attacks on U.S. soil. Part of him really wished there was a drone strike planned to take Kyung out, but the man who lived in the big white house had decreed they were to take him alive if possible. He heard a truck's engine approach.

"Be in there. Be in there," he whispered.

Ryan had to blink as his eyes dried out from staring too hard. A car door slammed. Footsteps crunched over dead leaves and semi-buried gravel.

"Hyuk?"

Ryan hit a remote. Paul's buddies at the NSA had rigged up a recording using isolated words from various recorded conversations with Hyuk Ch'oe. The result was quite impressive. It sounded just like Hyuk was responding to Shin when in fact the man lay unconscious inside the building. By the time Kyung realized this, it would be too late.

"Kyung present. Execute."

Suddenly the jungle came alive with men dressed in ghillie suits, surrounding Kyung and the building. One was so close Kyung would have tripped on him had he moved a foot to the left. Kyung spun in circles as the team encircled him. Ryan crawled out of his tree, weapon raised and trigger finger just a little itchy.

"Get on your knees!"

Kyung screamed something in Korean, and he pulled out a M67 fragmentation grenade. Several of the agents moved in, and the air filled with so many shouts that Ryan's ears rang. Kyung pulled the pin on the grenade, but an agent kicked it out of his hand.

It appeared time slowed to a crawl, but in a blink of an eye, Kyung was on the ground. Ryan wanted to verify with his own eyes that the man was finally in custody. Kyung burst up from the ground, screaming, then lunged. Ryan raised his weapon and for half a heartbeat thought about pulling the trigger but pistol-whipped Kyung across the face instead. He fell to the ground, and several of the agents tackled him. This time they hogtied him with cuffs and chains.

Ryan caught his breath as they loaded Kyung into a secured truck and led him away. It was over. But for so many recovering from the aftermath, their journey was just starting. The sound of the truck's engine faded, and Ryan couldn't help but listen until the last possible moment. He didn't quite trust the fact that the events of this week had concluded without further drama.

"So, we should probably go retrieve the sleeping asshole." Steven said.

"Or we could just leave him there. What's a worse punishment for his actions? Life in prison with all meals and recreation provided, or rotting slowly in a jungle and going mad from the isolation?"

"Personally, I'd choose option B, but unfortunately we do have to follow procedure, which includes due process. I can't thank you enough for your help, Ryan."

"Well, this has certainly been a vacation to remember."

"What are you going to do now? I mean you're off the hook for anything further on the investigation."

Ryan snorted. "You and I both know there will be task forces and inquisition I'll have to answer to in the coming months, but for right now ... I'm going back to my hotel, give my son a huge hug, fuck my husband and have a drink with my friends. Probably several drinks."

Steven shook his head. "TMI, man, but I was glad to hear that your friend will make a full recovery. How long will you be on the island?"

"Not sure. We are supposed to leave in six days, but we'll have to see."

"Well, if you want to grab a drink before you go, call me."

"Will do."

Ryan smiled and whistled a little tune as he walked down the dirt road toward a concealed truck that would take him back to civilization.

Chapter Fourteen

♥

"Alannah Nicole, don't taunt your brothers." Calleigh said as she sat down in one of the club chairs scattered around the hospitality suite. Their group had commandeered the top floor of the hotel since Ethan's return.

The kids were all gathered around the television watching something with lots of colors and annoying sounds. Ethan stood over by the wall of windows, staring out across the island.

"Think he's okay?" she asked Miranda.

"I hope so. He's seemed nervous ever since he got back from seeing Ryan."

Logan leaned in. "I think something is going down. He keeps checking his phone. And the way he gathered us all up, then led us away from our rooms? Why would he do that other than to make sure our group was in a central location and accounted for?"

Clay nodded. "It makes sense, but I haven't been able to get him to talk."

Vic handed Chase a bottle of water. "The news stations keep playing the same information over and over. All they keep saying is that it's a fluid situation. I didn't realize how much I hated that phrase until now."

Chase nodded. "I don't like just sitting here, waiting for news. But it's not as if any of us have the skills to help. Being out on the streets would most likely only complicate it for those trying to work the situation."

"Well, at least they're saying the number of casualties isn't near what they originally thought. I still can't help but feel guilty in a way." Miranda said.

"Why, Princess?"

"Well, in a few days we're all getting on a plane and flying away. But the people of this island have a long road to recovery and rebuilding ahead of them."

"I'm sure there are ways we can help. Just out of curiosity, have any of you contacted the airlines to find out if we *can* go home when scheduled? Last I heard, the airport is still closed." Vic said.

Calleigh leaned her head back on the chair and rested her eyes. She sighed as someone picked up her foot and massaged the arch. When she opened her eyes, she met Conor's aquamarine gaze.

It hardly seemed possible that their dream vacation that been turned upside down. She knew the kids were getting restless in the hotel, but so far the police were still asking residents and tourists to stay off the streets as much as possible.

If Ryan was involved in something at the moment, she really hoped it would bring some kind of conclusion to this stalemate of life.

Please let him be safe and come home to our family.

"I'm going to make the kids some supper in this nice little kitchen they have. Are any of you hungry?" Rick asked.

Calleigh shook her head. "No, I couldn't eat anything."

Rick looked over at Ethan. "Anything for you, Grapenuts?"

Ethan shook his head and checked his phone again. Then he spun around, and Calleigh didn't think she'd ever seen such a big smile on his face.

"I changed my mind. How about a champagne toast?"

Calleigh squinted as Ethan held up his phone. "What's it say?"

"It's over! They got the bastard."

"Earmuffs!" Michael and Brandon shouted together.

Calleigh jumped up so fast her head spun. Conor caught her, and her heart raced with exhilaration. The room swirled as Rick spun her around.

"Hey everybody, come look at this," Ethan yelled over by the windows.

She picked up Alannah and looked out. People filled the streets. Despite being twenty-five stories up, she felt their shouts of joy reverberate through her soul.

Rick sighed as the sun relaxed his muscles one by one. The entire island was breathing easier now that the man responsible for orchestrating the terrorist attacks was in custody. For the first time in days tourists and locals alike filled the white sandy beaches of Waikiki again, children shrieked as they ran in and out of the surf, and if he was being fanciful, he'd even say the island's breeze itself blew a happier rhythm.

"Feels gran' ter be our of dat hotel room again." Conor said.

Rick moaned as Conor kneaded a particularly tight muscle. "Yeah. Of course, that's not the only thing that feels good right now."

Conor kissed the back of Rick's neck. *"Ba mhaith liom tú anseo anois."* He whispered against Rick ear.

"Fuck, I love it when you do that. You realize if I stand up this family beach will become very indecent."

"I brought you both some water." Calleigh said as she sat on the chair beside them. "It looked like you were getting hot."

"In more ways than one *ár ghrá.*"

"Behave."

Rick and Conor both shook their heads, which of course made their wife roll her eyes. It was such fun to tease his angel. He looked out on the sand and watched Michael, Brandon, and Alannah playing in the sand. His family had gone through the most terrifying event of their lives and come out a stronger unit. He knew that had so much to do with their amazing group of friends.

"'Here come Chase an' his gang." Conor said.

Sure enough, Vic, Chase, Miranda, Charlie, and Gabriella were walking in their direction. Charlie took off down the sand, and Chase ran after him. His childish squeals of delight had Calleigh and Conor both chuckling.

Calleigh pointed in the opposite direction. "There's Ethan, Ryan, and Deshawn."

"Now all we're missing are—"

"You weren't going to say us, were you?" Clay said as he walked up behind them.

It seemed everybody had the same idea. Too bad Niall was still stuck in the hospital. Rick had taken the kids over to see him yesterday after they kept asking about where Niall, Uncle Matt, and Uncle Trevor were. At first he'd been worried that the kids would be scared at seeing

Niall in the hospital bed, connected to a bunch of wires and tubes. However, he should have known not to underestimate the maturity of his sons. Michael and Brandon had held Alannah's hands and explained that Uncle Niall needed to stay with the doctors so he could get better; then he would come home. The scene had almost every adult in the room choked up.

Logan and Clay set a cooler on the sand, then spread out their towels. Rick checked on the kids again and smiled as he saw Michael and Brandon sneaking up on Clay with a bucket of ocean water. Fortunately, they knew not to pull surprise attacks on Logan even with the waterproof setup on his speech processors. Logan backed away slightly, and Clay frowned. Rick looked at Vic, who held his hand over Gabriella's mouth so she couldn't shout a warning.

Conor tapped Rick on the shoulder. "Take squizz behind our wee covert agents."

Sure enough, Chase, Charlie, and Alannah were about to nail Michael and Brandon with the huge water cannons Trevor had bought the kids their first day on the island.

Clay turned right as Michael and Brandon tossed the bucket of water. Rick laughed as his friend caught a mouthful of seawater. Michael and Brandon gave each other high fives, but their cheers turned to yells as they received their own dousing.

Rick lunged out of the chair to join in the water fight. He grabbed a cannon of his own and ran for the surf. He jumped into the waves to fill the toy.

Conor ripped the plastic cannon from Rick's hand and tossed it up on the beach. "Aw no yer don't!"

Rick grabbed onto Conor as they tumbled into the water. He gripped his husband's waist and their legs tangled together. He needed some air, but when Conor's lips smashed against his, breathing became a forgotten necessity.

They surfaced together and looked up on the beach to see an all-out water fight had erupted between the adults and kids. Logan had taken up the position of general and was signing to the kids. Charlie tried to sign back, but it looked more like he was doing some kind of weird chicken dance.

"Think we should go help dem?" Conor asked.

Rick let the buoyancy of the salt water hold him up while Conor cradled him in his arms. He leaned his head back and watched his family enjoy the sun, sand and each other. This may not have been the vacation they all dreamed of, but he knew as long as they had each other, life would be a perfect adventure.

Epilogue

Boston Ten Weeks Later

Niall stepped off the elevator. It was the first time he'd seen their front door in almost two and a half months.

"You okay?" Trevor asked.

He turned and cupped the back of Trevor's head. Trevor blinked slowly, as if he'd just woken from a dream. Niall knew he would stare into those blue eyes for the rest of his life. Trevor was so beautiful in how he expressed his love for both him and Matt. Niall knew Matt stood only inches away from them, but this moment was for the man whose pure heart had done more to heal Niall from his injuries than any doctor could.

He grazed Trevor's jaw with his fingers; the roughness of his unshaven face tickled. His focus dropped to his thumb, where it brushed the very edge of Trevor's lower lip. Niall lowered his head and claimed Trevor's mouth. Trevor's arms came around his neck, and Niall couldn't think of a better noose. Groaning, Niall sank in deeper and kissed Trevor with every ounce of love inside him. He angled Trevor's head and slashed their open mouths together. He licked and probed.

A squeak from Trevor deepened to the rawest low moan Niall had ever heard. He dug his fingers into Trevor's scalp and ass cheeks, but he couldn't stop the flood of need roaring through his being. The need that only Trevor elicited.

"Maybe we should take this inside." Matt said, softly.

Niall heard the heat in Matt's voice and couldn't wait to stoke that fire till it consumed all three of them. He took his men's hands and led them to the front door. He wasn't entirely sure they'd actually make it to the bedroom. Niall used the keyed password to disengage the electronic lock and pushed the door open.

"Surprise!"

Niall froze. His heart racing in his recently repaired chest.

"Holy fuck!" Trevor yelled.

Everyone stood in their living room. Brandon and Michael laughed so hard they doubled over, and Vic, Chase, and Rick covered the youngest kids' ears. A huge sign welcoming them home was strung from one side of the room to the other.

Niall stepped forward and caught a racing Alannah in his arms. "Hello."

"You're home! Does that mean you're all better, Uncle Niall?"

"I'm mostly better, but I'm so glad to be back home with you."

"Guess what? We got cake and ice cream."

"Delicious. Will you share a piece with me?"

Alannah shook her head. "But I can get you your own."

"Gran' yer wee pipsqueak. Let de rest of us say hello." Conor said.

Conor picked up his daughter and slung her toward the group. Niall opened his arms, and Conor tentatively stepped into the embrace.

"I'm not going to break."

Conor tightened his arms. "*Nár laga Dia thú.* It means may God never weaken you."

Niall closed his eyes and gave thanks to *Manto* that he had such a special group of friends.

"I can't believe you guys are all here." Trevor said.

Logan waved, and Niall noticed a bit of hesitation in the greeting. Why would Logan feel unwelcome? The three of them had invited Logan and Clay over to their home many times.

"I'm so glad you are here." He signed.

Logan immediately started laughing and came closer.

"What? Did I say it wrong?" he asked.

Niall hadn't been the quickest study with sign language, but he tried. Generally, it felt as though he knew just enough to get himself in trouble.

"Well, that depends. Did you mean to say 'I'm bringing you a cigarette to play with your balls'?"

Niall groaned. "I think I actually get worse every time I try."

Logan put his hand on Niall's shoulder and gave it a squeeze. "It doesn't matter. That you even try means the world to me. I screw up all the time too. You should see me when I go to the support group meetings. Sometimes I feel like one of those wacky waving inflatable arm guys you see outside car dealerships. Now, judging by Matt and Trevor's expressions as you opened the door, our little surprise party might have been one big cockblock. I told Clay we should have given at least one of them a warning. So, sorry about that."

Matt stood with a glass of wine while talking to Rick. Trevor was getting one of the game systems going for the kids.

"Time with our friends is never something to apologize for. Besides Alannah said there's cake. That makes up for everything." He said, smiling and patted Logan's shoulder.

One of those glasses of wine looked like a good idea. He went over to the kitchen area. Calleigh stood at the island arranging some snacks. He saw her pause and grip the countertop for several seconds, then take several deep breaths. Niall rushed over and put his hand on her back.

"Are you well?"

Calleigh looked up and smiled. "I'm fine. It's just temporary."

Niall frowned. "If you're sick, you shouldn't be here. Get your husbands to take you home so you can rest."

"Oh, Niall, I'm fine. I just get these moments of dizziness some-times. They should go away in another couple of months."

"Another couple of ... wait are you—?"

Calleigh nodded and placed her hand on her lower stomach. "My doctor confirmed it shortly after we got back from the island. We should expect another little McGuire in October."

Niall took the petite woman in his arms and glanced over at Rick and Conor, who watched them with proud grins on their faces. When he let go, the smile on Calleigh's face lit up the room.

"I don't know much of my people's language, but I remember my grandparents saying a prayer when we learned someone in the tribe was expecting. May I say it for you?"

Calleigh's eyes filled with tears, and she nodded.

Niall took Calleigh's hands in his. "*Páhpohs pumôtamuwôk iyo kuc-shun.*"

"That was beautiful."

Niall looked around the room, but it seemed everyone's attention was focused elsewhere. "Have you told the others yet?"

She shook her head. "We were waiting until I crossed the thir-teen-week mark."

Niall looked around the room, which was filled with every person who was important to him. "You should do it now."

"But this is *your* welcome home party. We came here to celebrate your recovery."

"My recovery is about celebrating life, correct?"

Calleigh nodded.

"Then what could be better than announcing a new life to our family? It would be an honor to share this time with those we're closest to."

He picked up a glass of wine and winked at Calleigh. "Thank you so much for being here. I've known for many years that I was blessed to find such a wonderful group of friends. We love each other with a pure spirit, and I know that love has been a source of pleasure in times of joy and strength in times of trials. As individuals, we've grown and changed over the years, but our friendship has always been solid as the earth beneath our feet. Now within your hearts or out loud, I ask that you reflect upon the blessing of a new life that will soon join our family." He raised his glass. "Congratulations, clan McGuire."

The room erupted in cheers and exclamations of surprise. Niall sneaked away from the focus of everyone's attention. He found Matt and Trevor snuggled together on the large sectional.

"I'm pretty sure your words had everyone in the room entranced, *Caro.*" Matt said.

He looked around the room and smiled. "It's good to be home."

Leave a Review

♥

Thank you so much for reading An Imperfect Reunion. If you enjoyed this story, please leave a review to tell other readers how much you loved these characters. Sharing your reading experience with others on retailers and social media helps people find new reads and supports indie authors.

Thank you,

Trina Lane

Connect with Trina

- Website: www.trinalane.com

- Subscribe to my newsletter

- Email: trina@trinalane.com

- Facebook: trina.lane.books

- Facebook Group: Trina's Tantalizing Tales

- Instagram: @trina.lane.books

- Bluesky: @trinalane.bsky.social

Other Books by

Trina

♥

About Trina

♥

Trina is a scientist with a passion for history, music, and photography. She loves to travel and experience new places but is terminally shy around people she doesn't know. When the zombie apocalypse occurs, you'll want to find her because she's a crack shot, and promises to take out those nasty decomposing flesh-eating vermin before they have a chance to make you their snack. Her favorite aunt gave Trina a sultry romance novel to read while they were on vacation together back when Trina was in middle school and made her promise not to tell her mother. She's been hooked ever since! Her choices in reading and writing material are as diverse as her Apple Music library, which contains music from Mozart to Metallica. Her one concession is all stories must have a happily ever after ending—did we mention she's incurably romantic? She's the mother of a very strong-willed and sweet young man who frequently makes her smile and grimace within seconds of each other. She firmly believes that the sweetness comes from her, and the other part is her husband's fault. She loves to hear from readers and her greatest wish is that we all strive to achieve bigger dreams.